WHEN THE OCEAN CHANGED EVERYTHING

In memory of all those who lost their lives or were deeply impacted by the devastating disaster that shook us all on December 26, 2004.

The lives that were lost are irreplaceable; their memories and stories endure, like the ever-moving tide. For those of us who survived, each day is a step forward in carrying the weight of what was taken—a reminder of the lives cut short and the legacy we carry in their honor.

This is my truth, seen through the eyes of a 17-year-old caught in the chaos. It is a journey through fear, grief, and the echoes of that day that have reverberated through the years. What I share here are the memories etched in my heart—the images, emotions, and thoughts that have stayed with me, sometimes unwillingly, over time. Everyone who was there has their own truth. This is mine.

Out of respect for the individuals who stood by me or were present during those harrowing days, I have chosen to alter names and certain personal details. Memories, as they often do, have blurred and shifted over the years, and some parts of this story are told to give clarity where words might otherwise falter.

Let this serve as a collective remembrance—a tribute to the strength we found in one another, even in moments of unimaginable darkness. May the memories of those we lost inspire us with courage and love to continue moving forward.

Jenny Nirs

Jenny Nirs

WHEN THE OCEAN CHANGED EVERYTHING

My journey through disaster

Publisher: BoD · Books on Demand, Stockholm, Sweden
Print: Libri Plureos GmbH, Hamburg, Germany

ISBN: 978-91-8080-766-1

ONE

My hands trembled as I stared at the blinking Messenger call. I had been anticipating this moment ever since Chamali's unexpected friend request appeared on my Facebook days ago. Our brief, cautious exchanges had danced around the edges of familiarity, but each notification made time feel as though it had paused—like a thin crack forming in the silence and forgetfulness where I had long hidden my memories of Sri Lanka. Memories I wasn't sure I was ready to face.

My heart thudded heavily, each beat carrying a rush of conflicting emotions. Should I answer? How does one speak to someone they haven't spoken to in nearly twenty years? A friendship that had once meant the world now felt like a fragile thread tying me to a past I had deliberately buried.

After returning to Sweden, I had resisted every urge to search for Chamali. Reconnecting with her felt like reopening wounds I had spent years stitching closed. The memories of Sri Lanka were buried deep, sealed away in the unlit corners of my mind—safeguarded, yet ever-present.

Now, staring at the blinking screen, there was no escape. The call was a mirror, reflecting everything I had worked to suppress: the faces of those who hadn't survived, the terrifying chaos, and the quiet solace I had found in the company of Chamali and her family.

A tear slipped down my cheek before I could stop it. I wiped it away quickly, my fingers hovering over the screen, hesitating. Then, with a sigh that felt like a release, I pressed the button to answer.

December 13, 2004
Skärhamn, Sweden

It was early on Lucia morning, and the sky above the small coastal town of Skärhamn hung heavy and dark, as though the night was reluctant to surrender to the day. The cold stung my cheeks, and the wind tore through the empty streets, a harsh reminder of the Swedish winter we would soon leave behind. I shivered, tugging my sweater tighter around me. Despite layering two thick sweaters, the icy grip of winter still seeped through. My linen pants, meant for the tropical heat awaiting us, were no match for the biting cold, even with tights underneath.

We were traveling light—almost too light, given that we were about to journey across half the globe and be gone for more than a month. Four backpacks stood in a neat row against the wall by the bus stop. They seemed almost comically small, and I felt a twinge of both anticipation and uncertainty. The adventure ahead loomed large, surreal even. Here we were, standing in the quiet heart of familiar Skärhamn, the streets cloaked in night's shadow, yet within hours we would swap snow and frost for sand and sun. That warmth felt impossibly far away.

The square was still, wrapped in silence. The faint sound of waves brushing against the nearby shore reached my ears, and the dim glow of streetlights cast long, pale streaks on the ground. No cars rumbled by, no other footsteps echoed around us. It was just us—my family and I—poised to leave behind the darkness and chill for something entirely unknown.

"Let's hope we actually make it there with so little luggage," Dad muttered, stuffing his hands deeper into his jacket pockets. He eyed his lightly packed backpack and shook his head with a faint look of doubt.

"It'll be fine," Mom replied with a reassuring smile. "We'll pick up what we need once we're there."

My brother, Olof, shuffled impatiently, his boots scuffing the frost-bitten ground. His cheeks glowed red from the cold, though his restless energy betrayed his excitement. I followed his gaze to his pocket, where his new iPod was tucked securely. We had both received iPods as early Christmas presents, and they were already loaded with music for the long flight ahead. The sleek, futuristic devices felt like a piece of magic—something to carry us through the hours and make the journey even more thrilling.

"When will the bus arrive?" Olof asked impatiently, his breath visible in the chilly morning air.

"It's on its way," Mom replied with a thoughtful sigh, her gaze fixed down the dark road. And there, between the houses, we finally saw the faint glow of headlights cutting through the hazy morning mist.

The bus pulled up, its doors creaking open with a mechanical hiss. We loaded our backpacks into the luggage compartment, their dull thuds breaking the stillness, and climbed aboard. The worn seats embraced us with a kind of weary comfort, and soon the windows fogged up with our collective breath. I rested my head against the cold glass, watching the darkness outside gradually soften into the faint blue of dawn, though it was the kind of dawn that felt barely distinguishable from night.

The hum of the bus engine filled the silence as we rolled through the sleeping countryside. The low rumble, steady and rhythmic, seemed to lull everyone into their own thoughts. For me, it felt like the journey had already begun. Even though we were still on Swedish soil, I could feel the pull of the distant warmth waiting on the other side of the world.

When we arrived at Nils Ericson Terminal, the normally bustling hub lay eerily still. In the early morning hours, only a handful of travelers moved about, their rolling suitcases clicking softly against the tiled floors. Christmas decorations hung neatly across the space—red ribbons and sparkling lights glinting against the steel and glass—but instead of feeling festive, the scene reminded me of an empty stage awaiting its players.

We moved quietly through the hall, our steps echoing in the vast emptiness. Olof, always restless, fiddled with his iPod, his fingers brushing against it through his pocket, while Mom and Dad trailed behind, walking calmly with their backpacks slung over their shoulders.

As we passed under the high ceiling, something familiar caught my eye. Hanging among the holiday decorations were large photos of this year's Lucia candidates, their serene faces gazing down at the terminal below. My steps faltered when I recognized one of them. There, smiling softly from the center of the display, was Emelie, a girl I'd known in middle school. Draped in the traditional white Lucia gown with a crown of lit candles on her head, she seemed frozen in time, a stark contrast to the rushing reality of our morning.

"Isn't that Emelie?" Mom asked, following my gaze.

I nodded, a small smile tugging at my lips. "Yeah, that's her. How cool," I murmured, still surprised to see her up there, her image so polished and poised.

"She's beautiful," Mom said, her voice warm with admiration. "Is she this year's Lucia?"

"I guess so," I replied with a shrug, though I wasn't entirely sure. The thought stirred a bittersweet mix of jealousy and admiration. I envied her grace, her voice—something I lacked entirely. I followed my family through the terminal, stealing one last glance at her picture as we moved on, leaving Lucia crowns and snow behind for an adventure I couldn't yet fully grasp.

We moved on toward the next bus, the biting cold outside giving way to the cozy warmth inside as we headed to Landvetter Airport. The tension began to ease, and the anticipation of what lay ahead grew stronger.

At the airport, we prepared for the first leg of our journey. After passing through security, we boarded our first flight—a small propeller plane bound for Prague. I had imagined one of those grand jets parked on the tarmac, with wide aisles and rows of seats stretching endlessly. Instead, we were met by a plane that looked almost like a toy, its twin propellers humming loudly as we climbed aboard.

The seats were cramped, and the low ceiling made it feel as though the walls were closing in. I felt a flicker of nervousness as I settled into my seat, but it was quickly replaced by a tingle of excitement. Despite its size, this plane was the start of something much bigger—an adventure that had only just begun.

More passengers filed in, and the space felt even tighter. A basketball team filled several rows, their towering frames looking almost comical in the tiny seats. Across the aisle from me, one of the players struggled to fold his legs into the limited space, his knees nearly brushing his chest.

"This plane wasn't built for us," he muttered to his teammate, who nodded as he too tried to maneuver into a semblance of comfort.

I couldn't help but stifle a giggle, quickly covering my mouth to hide my amusement. Beside me, Olof leaned over and whispered, "Sometimes it's nice to be short." His deadpan delivery sent me into a fit of muffled laughter, and we exchanged amused glances as the plane began to taxi down the runway. Despite the discomfort, there was something endearing about the situation—it felt like an integral part of the journey.

When we landed in Prague, my dreams of tropical warmth were immediately dashed. A fierce wind swept across the tarmac, biting into my skin as thick snowflakes swirled through the air. It was colder here than it had been in Sweden, and I shivered as I pulled my sweater tighter around me.

"This wasn't exactly the plan," Mom said with a wry smile, the irony of our situation not lost on her.

"Good thing we'll soon be in Sri Lanka," Olof added, his voice tinged with hope. The warmth of his optimism did little to cut through the icy air, but it lifted my spirits nonetheless.

We hurried into the airport to escape the snowstorm, though the sense of limbo lingered—a frustrating pause on the way to something far more exciting. "Soon," I muttered, more to myself than anyone else.

Our overnight stay in Prague was anything but glamorous. Dad had booked a modest hotel near the airport—functional but far from cozy. The dimly lit corridors and worn furnishings gave the place a tired, lifeless feel. Snow continued to pelt the windows as we unpacked in our room, which was furnished with two hard beds, a creaky sofa bed, and a desk. The air felt damp and chilly, making it impossible to shake off the winter storm raging outside.

Wrapped in my thick sweater, I lay on the bed and stared at the foggy window, trying to summon visions of sunlit beaches and tropical breezes. It felt like an impossible dream in that moment.

"So, how's our tropical adventure shaping up so far?" Dad joked as he huddled under a blanket, his frozen hands tucked against his chest.

"Not quite as we imagined, but soon enough we'll be there," Mom replied in her usual reassuring tone.

"What do you say we grab something to eat?" she asked a little while later.

"No way!" I replied with a groan. The thought of braving the cold again made me want to burrow deeper under the covers.

"I saw a McDonald's just down the road," Mom coaxed. "We need to eat something."

Reluctantly, I agreed, and we bundled up once more to face the storm. As we trudged through the snow, I clung to the glimmer of hope that had carried us this far—a promise of the sun and warmth that lay just out of reach.

Back at the hotel later that night, I closed my eyes and tried to imagine the moment we'd finally step onto a sandy beach. I could almost feel the sun's warmth on my skin, hear the gentle lap of waves against the shore, and smell the salty

ocean air. It was a distant dream, but it was one that carried
me forward.

TWO

The screen flickered to life, and suddenly, there she was—a woman both familiar and yet so distant. Nearly twenty years had passed since we last heard each other's voices. Twenty years of silence and buried memories. For a moment, we sat quietly, gazing at one another through the cold lens of the screen. Time had softened the specifics, replacing them with hazy recollections, but there was still a flicker of heartfelt recognition.

Chamali looked older now. Her face, once youthful and radiant, had taken on sharper lines. Her cheeks were slightly sunken, and fine wrinkles marked her forehead—the undeniable traces of years gone by and, perhaps, the weight of all she had endured. But it wasn't only time that had left its mark; something deeper had shifted. Her dark, nearly black eyes still held their striking intensity, but they carried a gravity I couldn't quite define—an unmistakable depth that had grown over time. Her gaze was steady, confident, as if every gesture and movement was deliberate, each action a measured choice.

Her hair, once cascading over her shoulders in soft waves, was now tightly gathered into a bun at the nape of her neck. A streak of silver threaded through her jet-black hair, a vivid reminder of the years that had passed. Yet, it lent her an air of quiet dignity. Her strong, dark eyebrows framed her expression, a compelling mix of resolve and warmth.

She wore a crisp white shirt, perfectly tailored to her slender frame, its simplicity accentuating her composed and professional demeanor. Her posture was impeccable, almost commanding, projecting a calm confidence I hadn't expected.

But it was her smile that held me captive. Despite the passage of time, despite the changes etched by life and hardship, her smile was unchanged. Warm and radiant, it lit up her entire face, reaching her eyes and softening the angles of her features. It was a smile that seemed to bridge the years, pulling me back across two decades in an instant.

December 15, 2004
Bandaranaike International Airport, Sri Lanka

The sun blazed like a golden disc high in the sky as the plane touched down at Bandaranaike International Airport. Intense, warm light streamed through the windows, casting shadows across passengers' faces and filling the cabin with a vibrant energy. Anticipation bubbled in my chest as the plane began to slow.

"We're here!" Olof exclaimed, his grin wide as he pressed his nose to the window. His excitement was contagious, but I nudged him lightly. "Move over. I want to see too."

Mom's voice, ever the peacemaker, quickly followed. "Be nice to your little brother. Remember, this trip is about enjoying ourselves—no arguments, just sun, warmth, and swimming."

"And learning how to surf!" Dad, chimed in enthusiastically. Olof and I exchanged amused glances, laughing at Dad's eagerness to try a hobby he had yet to attempt.

"Safari!" Olof shouted, his voice brimming with excitement.

"And sampling the famous teas," Mom added, her interest in discovering new flavors always a priority.

"You can sip your tea while I snorkel," I replied with a grin, my eyes wandering over the tropical landscape beyond the window. Everything seemed alive here, pulsating with vibrant colors, rich scents, and radiant heat—a stark contrast to the wintery calm we had left behind in Skärhamn.

As we stepped off the plane onto the jet bridge, a wall of humid heat greeted us. It clung to my skin, thick and almost stifling, until we entered the cool haven of the arrivals hall. Bandaranaike International Airport was a gateway to a completely different world, its tropical air and the welcoming atmosphere of Sri Lanka immediately embracing us.

Christmas decorations were strung up everywhere—plastic garlands and multicolored baubles hung in stark contrast to the lush greenery and swaying palm trees visible through the windows. It felt surreal, almost comedic, to see such festive cheer against a tropical backdrop.

The airport buzzed with activity, a kaleidoscope of people from around the globe. Signs in Sinhala and English directed us through passport control and into the bustling baggage claim area. Vendors sold vibrant flower garlands and colorful sarongs along the hallways, their smiles and wares adding to the sensory overload. This was Sri Lanka—vivid, alive, and unlike anything I'd ever experienced.

Airports have a distinct energy, a mix of excitement and tension as people either rush toward new destinations or arrive at long-awaited ones. Among the sea of travelers, I couldn't spot another Swede. It gave me a small thrill, as if we were explorers stepping into uncharted territory, our language a secret code in this unfamiliar place.

Mom, Karin, squinted at the signs, muttering translations under her breath. I couldn't help but laugh softly. Thankfully, the English translations were easy enough to follow.

At the baggage carousel, the wait began. "It'd be just our luck if the luggage didn't show up," Dad grumbled, his tone teasing but with an edge of worry.

"Maybe it's still stuck in the snowstorm in Prague," Olof joked, nudging me in the side. The thought of the freezing snowstorm we had left behind sent a shiver down my spine, but the oppressive heat of Sri Lanka quickly reminded me we were far from that icy world now.

Finally, the carousel jerked to life, and backpacks began to appear. "There they are!" Mom called out, hurrying forward. One by one, we retrieved our modest luggage—four backpacks filled with only the essentials for a month-long adventure.

We exited the airport, and the transition from the cool, air-conditioned terminal to the outdoor heat was like stepping into a sauna. The humidity was intense, wrapping around me like a heavy blanket, and each breath felt thick and warm. I glanced at Mom, who handed me a bottle of water she had wisely purchased inside. Gratefully, I took a few deep gulps, the icy liquid soothing my parched throat.

Outside the doors, rows of yellow taxis stretched as far as the eye could see, their drivers shouting and waving energetically to attract the attention of arriving tourists. A thrill of excitement coursed through me as I took in the scene, the lively energy of a place that felt so completely different from anything I had known.

We piled into a taxi bound for Colombo, the bustling capital of Sri Lanka. Dad claimed the front seat and immediately struck up a conversation with the driver, a wiry man named Kumar. With animated gestures and a wide smile, Kumar eagerly answered Dad's barrage of questions about local attractions and the best surfing spots, all while maneuvering skillfully through the city's chaotic traffic.

The streets were alive with movement. Cars and buses jostled for space in a symphony of honking horns, while mopeds and tuk-tuks darted through the gaps, weaving in patterns that seemed random yet strangely synchronized.

Every so often, Dad would glance at the map spread across his lap, his brow furrowed. "I think he's taking us on the scenic route to make a bit of extra cash," he muttered over his shoulder, his suspicion clear.

"And how would you know that?" Olof shot back with a smirk. "You've never even been here before!"

"Exactly," Dad replied, clearly irritated, eliciting a quiet chuckle from Mom.

"Look at all the spices!" Mom exclaimed, her eyes lighting up as she pointed to the vibrant market stalls that lined the roadside. Piles of colorful spices spilled over the edges of their containers, creating a striking contrast to the bustling chaos around them.

Colombo welcomed us in a whirlwind of colors, sounds, and scents. The streets buzzed with life, a never-ending flow of activity. Vendors stood proudly behind makeshift stalls brimming with fragrant spices, glistening fruits, and intricately crafted jewelry, their voices raised in calls to passing locals and tourists. The city felt like it moved to its own rhythm—a chaotic symphony of life in perfect disarray.

As the taxi navigated the narrow streets, Kumar pointed out landmarks and historic sites, his voice filled with pride as he introduced us to his city. My eyes darted from one sight to the next: fruit and spice markets overflowing with color, flashing neon signs advertising shops in languages I couldn't read, goats and cows wandering leisurely through the throng, and an endless stream of people, each with their own purpose. The sheer energy of it all was intoxicating, overwhelming in the best way.

There were no crosswalks in sight, and it seemed as if traffic rules were more of a suggestion than a standard. Yet Kumar drove with effortless confidence, navigating the chaos with a calm that suggested he knew these streets like the back of his hand. I leaned back in my seat, trying to take it all in, knowing that this moment—this first, vibrant glimpse of Sri Lanka—would stay etched in my memory for a lifetime.

THREE

I stared at the screen as memories washed over me, like a wave retreating only to surge back with relentless force. The tightness in my chest was the same as it had been that day when everything began. It felt as if the entire world had frozen in an uncanny stillness. I remembered that moment vividly—the silence before the storm, a foreboding calm that left me paralyzed with dread. Then, in an instant, everything shattered.

Chamali's smile on the screen blurred as the memory overtook me—I saw myself on the roof of a bus, screaming for help, struggling to breathe as torrents of water swept away everything and everyone. The sound of those screams echoed in my mind—screams from people losing their homes, their loved ones, their lives. It was a sound that had etched itself into my soul, one I could never unhear.

I shook my head as if to shake off the weight of the past that clung to me like wet sand. I was home now, safe in the familiar walls of my house, yet the flood of emotions felt just as potent as it had back then. The panic, the sorrow, the guilt—they surged through me, raw and unrelenting. I had survived, but countless others had not.

In the distance, the laughter of my children rang out, light and joyful, filling the room with a warmth that contrasted sharply with the storm raging inside me. Their giggles were a lifeline, pulling me back to the present, but I knew there were things I could never share with them—memories too heavy, too dark to burden them with. And now, as Chamali sat smiling at me through the screen, the weight of it all came crashing down again, catching me off guard.

The guilt resurfaced, as it always did. Why had I been spared? Why had I come home, built a life, had children, while others lost everything? There were no answers, no logic to cling to—just an aching, unshakable injustice. I drew a shaky breath, desperate to steady myself. I wanted to live in the now, to be strong for my family, but that day had left an indelible mark, a scar that would never truly fade.

Another deep breath. I forced myself back into the present, back to Chamali's gaze on the screen. Her smile was steady, grounding. We had both survived, somehow, and despite the years of silence and the miles that had separated us, we had found our way back to each other.

December 15, 2004
Colombo, Sri Lanka

The taxi stopped in front of a grand hotel by the sea, and we stepped out, slightly unsteady after the long journey. The ocean breeze greeted us immediately, carrying a warm, humid embrace that wrapped around me like a tropical blanket.

"It barely cost anything," Dad said with a satisfied smile, shutting the taxi door after paying the driver. His expression quickly shifted as he turned to take in the impressive hotel. "But this place will cost a fortune," he muttered, eyeing the building warily.

The hotel was magnificent—a gleaming white colonial-style structure with towering pillars and arched windows. The entrance was framed by lush palm trees, their fronds swaying gently in the breeze. A row of lanterns lined the pathway to the grand double doors, giving the place an air of old-world charm, as if every corner held a story waiting to be told.

"I don't get why we needed a place like this," Dad grumbled, but his words went unnoticed as Mom strode confidently toward the entrance.

"It's nice to have everything sorted for our first night," Mom replied with a contented smile. Two young men in crisp uniforms appeared as if on cue, swiftly taking our backpacks with effortless grace, adding to the seamlessness of the experience.

Inside, the reception area was dazzling. High ceilings adorned with ornate crystal chandeliers cast shimmering reflections across the checkered marble floor. The air was cool and carried a faint floral scent, likely from the meticulously arranged bouquets scattered throughout the room.

The receptionist greeted us with a practiced smile and a slight bow. She spoke with polished professionalism, explaining the hotel's amenities before handing over our room keys.

"Come and look at this!" I called excitedly after wandering through the reception to the terrace. The view stopped me in my tracks. From the veranda, the Indian Ocean stretched endlessly before me, its waves crashing rhythmically against the rocks below.

A cooling sea breeze swept across my face, and I felt the fatigue of the journey fade. Standing there, with the sun warming my skin and the ocean's vastness filling my view, I was struck by a sense of awe and exhilaration.

"Wow!" Olof exclaimed as he joined me, his face lighting up with the same mix of excitement and wonder. "Where can we swim?" he asked, brushing the sweat off his forehead.

"Let's take the bags to the room first, and then we'll figure it out," Mom said cheerfully, gesturing toward the grand staircase. Her light footsteps echoed on the marble floor as we followed her upstairs.

Dad handed me and Olof a heavy key with an engraved wooden fob. "You two are sharing," he said with a grin. Olof snatched the key and raced ahead.

"Window seat is mine!" I shouted after him, laughing as I climbed the stairs.

When I reached the room, Olof had left the bed closest to the window for me. I dropped my backpack onto the soft white duvet and glanced out the window. The view was as stunning as I had hoped—the endless ocean sparkling in the afternoon sun.

Olof was already in his swim trunks, bouncing impatiently. "Hurry up!" he urged, grinning from ear to ear.

"Go ahead, I'll catch up," I replied, digging through my backpack for my swimsuit. I changed quickly and threw on a breezy yellow dress before slipping into my flip-flops.

Back downstairs, Mom was waiting by the reception. "Dad and Olof went toward the garden," she said, pointing the way. We followed a cobblestone path flanked by neatly trimmed bushes and vibrant tropical flowers. The scent of the blooms mingled with the salty air, creating an intoxicating blend that made everything feel new and alive.

The path led us to a break in the stone wall surrounding the hotel grounds, where a staircase descended to a small, secluded beach. The view took my breath away, but something else caught my attention.

"Mom, you've got to see this!" I called, pointing to a large sign near the staircase.

She looked puzzled until her eyes found the sign: "SEA UNSAFE!"

With a laugh, I snapped a photo just as Dad and Olof splashed happily in the crystal-clear water, completely ignoring the warning.

"John!" Mom called out in exasperation. "Did you see the sign?"

"What sign?" Dad called back, his voice echoing against the rocks.

"The one that says the ocean might be dangerous," I teased, still laughing.

Mom frowned. "It's not funny. What if it really is dangerous?"

Dad waded back to shore, shrugging. "It's probably just the currents. We'll stick close to the beach."

We sat at the water's edge, digging our toes into the soft, warm sand. Cool waves lapped at our feet, relaxing us, as if the ocean itself was welcoming us. I watched as Mom closed her eyes and tilted her face toward the brilliant sun. It was as if all the tension and fatigue from the journey melted away the moment she sank into the sand.

"Think of the adventure we're going to have," she said, her voice carrying a note of relaxation. But suddenly, she opened her eyes and stared at my shoulders.

"Oh no! We haven't put on sunscreen!" She pressed her thumb lightly against my shoulder.

"You'll turn as red as a lobster if we sit here without sun protection," she continued, her voice teetering between teasing and serious.

Dad sighed and stood up. "It's about time for food anyway," he said, brushing sand off his hands. "Let's head back before we get sunburned."

We climbed the stone stairs back to the hotel, the sun dipping lower on the horizon. Despite the brief swim and the scolding about sunscreen, the promise of adventures to come hung in the air like the warmth of the setting sun.

FOUR

I shook off the memories and returned to the present. Chamali's laughter resonated through the slightly crackly connection, carrying with it a contagious warmth. To my surprise, I found myself laughing too, as though releasing a small part of the burden I had carried for so long. I found myself caught in a strange mix of past and present, but hearing Chamali's laughter, I couldn't help but smile.

"Hello, my dear! It's been so long!" Chamali exclaimed, her voice as light and cheerful as I remembered from all those years ago, as if we were back on the street outside their house, laughing together as we played badminton. It felt almost surreal to hear her voice again, a reminder of everything we had been through.

"Hello, Chamali! How are you?" I heard my own voice, slightly trembling, yet filled with joy. It felt as though time had drawn a sharp line between then and now, but despite that, there was a connection between us that was impossible to sever. Something in Chamali's voice was so familiar, something that took me back to

another time—right to the moment when the world crumbled beneath our feet.

It was strange. Familiar, yet so foreign. Our lives had taken such different paths. The last time we saw each other, we had been 17—young and naïve, but with a newfound awareness of life's brutal reality. Back then, we had no idea how our lives would unfold or that our meeting would become a scar we'd carry for the rest of our lives.

I remembered the days after the disaster, when we had clung desperately to fragments of normalcy amidst the chaos. We laughed, told stories, and sought small moments of joy, even as everything around us lay in ruins. We didn't realize it at the time, but those experiences were carving themselves into us, shaping who we would become. Every scream, every shattered body, every stormy night became ingrained in us, woven into the very fabric of who we are.

December 15, 2004
Colombo, Sri Lanka

I followed the rest of the family as they weaved between shops and street stalls lining the road. The warm afternoon had made all of us slather on generous amounts of sunscreen, leaving our skin glistening slightly in the tropical light. Dad had declared tonight's mission to be of the utmost importance: finding a sunhat. He was convinced he would burn his ears off if he didn't find one immediately.

"I won't survive this sun without a hat!" he muttered, wiping his already sweaty forehead.

"There might be something over there," I said, pointing to a large department store with a glass entrance, where the promise of air conditioning offered a welcome relief.

"Wait!" Dad suddenly shouted, grabbing my arm just as a large truck packed with goats thundered past us on the street. "My God, the way they drive!" he exclaimed, pointing toward a crosswalk further down the road, where cars, mopeds, and tuk-tuks zigzagged through the chaotic, bustling traffic. "You've got to stay alert out here."

It was late afternoon, and we had been wandering through the central parts of the city for hours. The streets here were slightly more organized than the narrow alleys we had explored earlier—there were even crosswalks and traffic lights, though no one seemed particularly interested in following them. Vehicles and pedestrians jostled for space everywhere, and the city's sounds—a cacophony of honking cars, vendors shouting, and the hum of mopeds—formed a constant background noise.

After carefully crossing the street, instinctively clutching onto one another's arms, we finally stepped into the department store. The cool air hit us like a refreshing breeze, and it felt as if we had stepped into an entirely different world. Inside, Christmas decorations were everywhere. Garlands and blinking ornaments hung from the ceiling, and in the center of the building stood a massive, decorated Christmas tree. Once again, the contrast between the tropical heat outside and the glittering holiday decorations felt incredibly surreal.

"I've found it!" Dad suddenly exclaimed and, without waiting for the rest of us, strode off toward a shop on the right. My brother and I looked after him in surprise. In the window hung a selection of sunhats, and I couldn't help but laugh at their appearance. They were large and clunky, in garish colors that clashed horribly, with wide brims that looked like they could catch every gust of wind passing by.

"Those are probably the ugliest sunhats I've ever seen," I said, shaking my head with a laugh.

"Let's go into this store instead," I suggested, pulling my brother into the shop next door. It was filled with surf shorts, branded t-shirts, and flip-flops in every imaginable color and pattern. The Quicksilver brand dominated the displays, and it was exactly the type of clothing that made Olof's eyes light up. He immediately began sifting through the racks, and I joined in.

By the time Dad and Mom joined us, I was already standing by the fitting rooms, fully occupied with picking out clothes for both myself and my little brother. "Mom, you said we should pack light so we could buy clothes when we got here!" I called out enthusiastically, holding up a pair of brightly colored shorts. "Everything here is so cheap!"

Mom laughed at my excitement. "Yes, I did say that," she admitted, nodding approvingly at Olof, who emerged from the fitting room wearing a blue-gray patterned Quicksilver t-shirt. "But don't buy the whole store now." Her lighthearted tone slightly tempered the obvious enthusiasm in me and Olof, but we still couldn't resist filling our baskets with bargains.

"This is daylight robbery!" muttered Dad behind us. He was back to his usual grumbling about money, which he often did when too much was being spent. Yet he couldn't quite hide a small smile when he saw how happy we were.

After half an hour of trying on clothes and bargaining, we were back on the warm, bustling street. The sun had dipped lower in the sky, but the heat still pressed down heavily. Dad pulled out his newly purchased sunhat—a blue one featuring Sri Lanka's iconic golden lion. "Now, aren't you all a little jealous?" he said smugly as he put it on. We laughed heartily, but I could feel the energy from earlier starting to wane. What had started as a fun outing had turned into a tired slog, and the cheerful chatter that had filled the store earlier was now fading into a more subdued silence.

"We need food," Mom declared, taking a deep breath. Beads of sweat glistened on her forehead, and it was clear that both hunger and fatigue were taking their toll.

"Yeah, but where should we eat?" Olof asked, glancing around as if expecting the perfect restaurant to appear out of nowhere.

The bustling crowds and traffic were still all around us. The street stalls, once enticing with their scents and colors, now felt like obstacles to avoid rather than experiences to enjoy. My feet felt heavy, and Olof looked as tired as I felt. The long journey was catching up with us, and we needed to find somewhere to sit, somewhere to refuel before the evening ended.

After what felt like an eternity of wandering through the streets, we finally stumbled upon a narrow side alley. It was quiet and less chaotic than the main thoroughfare we'd been exploring, but it had a certain charm. The stalls and shops looked worn, but the fragrant steam rising from a food stall further down the street immediately caught our attention.

Nestled between two dilapidated buildings, under an almost invisible sign with peeling paint, was a modest eatery. It was clear that the place had seen better days. Some of the tables on the sidewalk were rust-stained, and the chairs looked wobbly. Yet there was something about the atmosphere—something genuine and welcoming. Or maybe it was simply our hunger speaking. The aromas coming from the small kitchen were intense and inviting; a blend of spices I had never encountered before filled the air, making my stomach growl loudly.

"What do you think about trying here?" Dad asked, nodding toward the little restaurant, barely able to hide his curiosity about what it had to offer. We stopped and looked at one another to assess the option. None of us were in the mood to keep searching, so we all nodded in agreement.

We settled at one of the tables, which wobbled slightly as we sat down. The chairs were uneven, and I felt it tilt under my weight.

When the menu arrived, written in Sinhala with faded ink on a laminated sheet, we weren't entirely sure what to expect. But the waiter, a young man with a warm smile, pointed to a few dishes and did his best to explain in broken English what they were. We were a bit uncertain about what we'd actually ordered, but our moods were already improving.

When the food arrived, steaming hot and vibrantly colorful, it was as if the day's fatigue melted away. The plates were filled with aromas and flavors I had never experienced before. Each bite was an explosion of spices and textures—a mix of chili heat, the sweetness of coconut milk, and the fresh tang of lime leaves. The roti bread was soft and buttery, perfect for dipping into the rich sauces. It was food that warmed us from the inside and replenished us with new energy.

Despite the eatery's humble appearance, this turned out to be the best meal of the trip so far. Initially skeptical, I found myself taking large bites, smiling contentedly. "This is really good," I mumbled between mouthfuls, and the others nodded in agreement.

We lingered at the little eatery, leaning back and savoring the moment. After hours of wandering, it was a relief to simply sit, enjoy delicious food, and let the tropical heat slowly cool as the sun set. The glow of streetlights began to glimmer in the humid evening air, and from the small kitchen came the soft clinking of dishes and pans.

None of us were in a hurry to leave. We shared the last pieces of roti bread, laughed about how we had only visited one shopping center yet managed to find everything we needed for the trip, and planned what to do next. The atmosphere was relaxed, filled with relief at finally being recharged.

When we eventually stood to leave and stepped back into the evening, we felt somehow closer—not just to each other but to the place we were in. We had tasted a piece of Sri Lanka, not just through its food but through the quiet charm of a little side alley where life flowed on, away from the bustling tourist streets.

FIVE

"Darling! Everything is good!" Chamali's voice broke through my memories, pulling me back to reality. "I'll show you," she continued in her slightly broken English. With the phone in hand, she stepped back toward the wall behind her and proudly displayed a row of photographs hanging there.

I leaned in, squinting at the screen. There, in the photos, I saw Chamali, her sister Anjali, and the rest of their family. They were smiling at the camera, their faces carrying a kind of newfound strength. I saw reflections of myself in their faces, yet there was something new, something that spoke of a life filled with struggle and determination. Chamali also showed me a photo where she and her sister were dressed in military uniforms. I stared at the image, almost unable to believe my eyes.

"Wow, you followed in your father's footsteps!" I exclaimed in surprise.

"Yes," Chamali replied proudly. "But I went further. I'm an officer now," she continued, explaining that even her younger sister, Anjali, was now studying to become an officer in the Sri Lankan Army. It was surreal to hear about this life—so different from my own, yet so clearly intertwined with our shared past.

It felt unreal. Here we were, the same age, yet our life journeys couldn't have been more different. I had built a stable life with a family, children, a job, and a home. Chamali had stayed, built her life around her family and her country, training to protect and defend. We had chosen completely different paths, and our lives were polar opposites.

A weight settled over my chest, a mix of sorrow and longing for what could have been, but also a deep respect for the strength I saw in my friend's face.

December 16, 2004
Mirissa, Sri Lanka

The day started early, after a delicious breakfast at the hotel in Colombo. We decided to spend the morning enjoying the garden and pool near the hotel before having lunch there and continuing our adventure. We'd been given a tip about a small place at the southernmost end of Sri Lanka, called Mirissa. According to the receptionist, it was supposed to be something truly special, and that's where we were heading that day. The friendly receptionist had arranged for a taxi to pick us up shortly after lunch.

The hotel's lunch buffet was a delight—filled with fresh fruit, freshly baked roti bread, and flavorful curries that gave us a final taste of Colombo before we set off. The food was exactly what we needed to gather strength for the long drive south. The city had already been cloaked in a humid heat that seemed to grow more intense as the day went on, with the air heavy and sticky.

When we finally got into the minibus and started our journey, we rolled down the windows, hopeful for a refreshing breeze. It was in vain. The farther south we drove along the coast, the more the weather began to change. The heat lingered, but the sky shifted—the clear blue tones gave way to a gray blanket of clouds. The air felt charged, and as we approached Mirissa, the weather grew dramatic. Dark clouds rolled in over the coast, and in the distance, we could see heavy rain falling over the ocean.

By the time we neared our destination, the rain was pounding against the minibus windows, and the wind whipped at the palm fronds along the road. It was late afternoon, but it felt like night. The rain fell so heavily that we could barely see the road ahead.

The patter of rain mixed with the monotonous hum of the minibus engine, creating an almost hypnotic effect. There was something numbing about it all—the weather, the darkness, the creeping exhaustion that enveloped us.

Mom sat quietly beside me, her eyes closed, her hand pressed against her temple. Her migraine had set in early during the trip, and I could see how each jolt of the road worsened her pain. Every time the minibus hit a pothole, she took a sharp, pained breath and sighed heavily. I glanced at her, worried about how she would manage. Her face was tense, and it was clear the migraine was taking over.

We hadn't booked any accommodations in advance—it had originally felt like part of the adventure. The plan was to travel on instinct, finding hidden gems along the way and living in the moment. But now, with rain hammering against the windows and darkness enveloping us like a heavy shroud, it felt less like an adventure and more like a desperate race against time, the elements, and our own exhaustion.

When we arrived at the first place we found, it looked more like a treehouse than a hotel. Nestled among some palm trees, it was built on rough planks with a roof made of what appeared to be palm leaves. It was hardly inviting, but at that moment, we had no other choice. We stepped out of the minibus, and within seconds, we were soaked from head to toe. It was as if the rain had been waiting for us, ready to greet us with all its force. Our feet sank into the muddy ground as we approached the treehouse, and I felt the rain seep through my clothes.

Under the dim light of a few hanging bulbs, we saw a group of young surfers gathered in a circle, enveloped in a haze of smoke. The smell of their joints mixed with the humid air and rain, and they looked as if they didn't have a single care in the world. On the wall behind them hung a large, faded poster of Bob Marley. They looked like living copies of him—long dreadlocks, colorful bandanas, laid-back and almost dreamy expressions. Music from a portable speaker played a soft, slow reggae rhythm that blended seamlessly with the rhythmic fall of the rain.

"Heeey," one of them greeted lazily as we approached. His voice was as relaxed as the rest of him, and it didn't seem to matter to him that it was raining or that we stood there completely soaked. Their world felt worlds apart from ours at that moment.

Mom let out a deep sigh, and even though her eyes stayed closed, I could see the discomfort etched in her furrowed brow. I knew she wasn't feeling well, and being here only seemed to make it worse. She held her backpack tightly, as if trying to gather her thoughts.

"We can't stay here," she said firmly, without even opening her eyes to look at us. It wasn't just the rain or her migraine—this wasn't what we had envisioned.

"But shouldn't we stay just one night so you can recover from the migraine?" Dad asked cautiously, rubbing her back gently. I could hear the concern in his voice, and I knew he was just trying to make things easier for her. We were drenched after only a short time outside, and staying for the night would at least mean we'd have a roof over our heads. But I already knew Mom wouldn't agree.

She slowly turned toward the rest of us. Her face was tired and full of pain, but there was a determination in her gaze that made it clear none of us would challenge her. She shook her head, a small and weary no. None of us said anything; we simply followed her lead, unquestioning. Without needing to say a word, we all understood that we would move on.

"Yo man! Check out that place," one of the Bob Marley lookalikes called out, pointing with his joint toward a white wall further down the street. We thanked him, turned around, and stepped back out into the rain.

The rain continued to pour relentlessly, and the darkness felt almost tangible as we returned to the street. We trudged onward in the direction he had pointed, wet and stiff from a day spent in the car, clinging to a faint hope that we would find something better up ahead.

The rain still fell in heavy, thick streams. Mom, with her migraine, looked increasingly strained. As we approached the white wall further down the street, we found a place that seemed far more inviting than the treehouse we had seen earlier. It was like stumbling upon a small oasis in the middle of the storm. The bungalows were proper buildings, with solid walls and roofs—a sign that we could finally have a night in safety and dryness. The place was nestled in a lush garden that appeared magical despite the rain. String lights twinkled through the downpour, casting a soft, golden glow over the swaying silhouettes of palm trees. There was a kind of peace here, a sense that we had, at least temporarily, found a home.

Mom, who seemed to be fighting to keep her eyes open, sighed with relief when she saw the clean, simple bungalows. "We can stay here," she said softly, leaning heavily on Dad, who guided her to the reception. I looked at her and realized she was completely drained, both physically and mentally, after the day's trials. But for the rest of us, the feeling was different—we were tired, sure, but the excitement of having arrived and the anticipation of what the next day might bring was much stronger.

After checking in, we hurried into our bungalows to escape the humid weather. The rooms were simple but clean, and the smell of wood and moisture mixed with the tropical air wafting in through small open windows. Mom collapsed onto the bed immediately, grateful to finally rest, while the rest of us took the time to inspect every corner. There was something exciting about this place, something that sparked our imaginations despite the rain drumming on the roofs.

Olof and I exchanged a look of eager anticipation. We could hardly wait to explore the garden, the beach, and perhaps meet the locals. Going to bed felt like opening the first window of an advent calendar—we knew something amazing awaited us, but we had to wait until morning.

There was a tension in the air, as though we stood on the threshold of something big. The unknown, hidden behind the night's darkness and rain, filled us with anticipation. Despite our exhaustion, the thought of what we might discover the next day was enough to keep us awake a little while longer.

The rain continued to fall outside, the wind whispered through the palms, and we could hear the ocean's roar in the distance. Even though we couldn't see the beach yet, we knew it was there, just a stone's throw away, waiting for us when the morning light finally broke through the clouds. We could hear the waves crashing against the shore.

As Olof and I stepped into our bungalow, the rain still pattered against the roof, but it no longer bothered us. Now, we were indoors, dry and safe. I threw my backpack down and started unpacking when I heard a strange noise near the door. It sounded like something scraping against the ground outside. At first, I thought it was just the wind playing with some branches, but when I looked closer, I saw something moving slowly across the veranda.

"What's that?" I asked, pointing toward the door. My heart suddenly beat faster, and a gnawing unease rose in me.

Olof came over, and we looked together. There, right by the threshold, was a large hermit crab slowly crawling forward. "Look! A hermit crab!" Olof exclaimed, as if it was the most exciting discovery in the world. I jumped back in surprise. It was enormous—much larger than any hermit crab I'd ever seen before. Even though I had encountered hermit crabs many times before, and Olof and I used to collect them at the beach when we were kids, this was something entirely different. The hermit crab's shell glistened wetly in the light from the veranda, and its claws lightly scraped the wooden floor. It seemed almost as curious about us as Olof was about it.

Olof picked it up, fascinated, to get a closer look. It was nearly the size of his hand. He laughed out loud when he saw the look on my face. "If you think this guy is scary, wait until you see the others!" he said gleefully, stepping off the veranda.

Around our bungalow were several more large hermit crabs, as if they were standing guard. They slowly crawled over the rocks, blending seamlessly into their surroundings. It felt as if they were part of the nature here—a reminder that we were now far from everything familiar.

Listening to the rain drumming on the roof, smelling the damp earth, and watching the hermit crabs quietly move around made the place feel like an adventure in itself. At the same time, it felt comforting. Here, we were sheltered from the weather, surrounded by nature's quiet inhabitants, and finally able to recover from the journey.

I lay down on the bed with a sense of excitement and anticipation—tomorrow would reveal what this place truly had to offer when daylight finally broke through the heavy rain clouds.

SIX

"Do you still live in the same house?" I asked, finally feeling like I was regaining my composure. We had been talking for a few minutes now, after all these years, and every word felt like a step back in time. Now that the initial shock of hearing Chamali's voice had subsided, I dared to ask more.

"Yes, same house!" Chamali replied with a smile before turning the camera toward the room around her. I stared at the screen, and suddenly I was there again—in the same living room where I had spent so many hours during those intense days. I recognized every little detail. The furniture was still simple, a mix of wood and fabric, worn by time but well cared for. The same family photos hung on the walls, framed in exactly the same way I remembered.

It was as if time had stood still in that house, even though 20 years had passed. The memory of the room was so vivid, as if it were only yesterday that I had sat there with Chamali's family. And now, once again, I felt that strange mix of fascination and distance.

I remembered the dinners we had eaten there—almost ritualistic experiences that felt so far from the life I live now. I could see myself sitting at the table; the guests and the eldest family members always ate first. The daughters and the mother ate last.

It was so different from what I was used to. I thought back to my own upbringing, where meals had been loud and full of chatter and laughter, where everyone ate at the same time and no one cared if someone grabbed an extra serving before someone else. That tradition had carried on into my own family, where I always felt happiest when the table was crowded with people.

At first, I hadn't known what to do during those dinners at Chamali's house, but I had adapted. There was no choice.

December 17, 2004
Mirissa, Sri Lanka

The days that followed were some of the best I had ever experienced. Every morning, stepping out of our bungalow, I was greeted with the same feeling—as if I were living in a dream. The white sandy beach and crystal-clear water seemed almost unreal in their perfection. But what truly made the place special were the people who ran the small restaurant and the bungalows.

The restaurant owner, Dilan, was always there every morning. His face lit up whenever he saw us arrive, as if we were old friends returning each day. "Good morning, my friends!" he would always greet us, his broad smile revealing white teeth against his sun-weathered skin. He was an older man, with a body that bore the marks of a life of hard work, yet there was a calmness and confidence in his movements that only someone with deep experience could have.

"Dilan," I asked one day as we sat drinking our morning smoothies, "how long have you had this place?"

He pulled up a chair beside us, settling in as if he had been waiting for the perfect moment to share his story. "It was a long time ago," he began, his gaze drifting over the tranquil beach. "Back then, there was nothing here—just empty land and the endless sea." He gestured toward the row of bungalows behind us. "All of this," he continued, "we built with our own hands, one stone at a time. It was no easy task, but we believed in what we were creating. We knew it would be worth it."

Just then, Amara, his wife, stepped out of the kitchen, smiling warmly at us. "We started with just one bungalow," she said, wiping her hands on her apron. "It took us years to save enough to build the next one. We wanted each bungalow to be perfect, so every guest would feel at home here."

She explained that they had dreamed of building something of their own ever since they got married. "We wanted something that was ours, something we could pass down to our children one day," Amara said as she slowly stirred a pot of coconut milk for breakfast. They had two children, a son and a daughter, who lived in Colombo and worked in the hospitality industry. "They learned everything here," Dilan said proudly. "Now they help manage larger hotels, but they always come home to us when they have time off."

At one point, Mom asked how they managed the daily workload of running the restaurant, tending to the gardens, and taking care of guests. "We've done this for so long it's just part of who we are," Amara said with a laugh. "I love being in the kitchen. And seeing people enjoy the food we prepare—it makes it all worthwhile."

Aside from Dilan and Amara, Ravi, their young chef, was an indispensable part of the operation. Ravi was quiet and often stayed in the kitchen, but we occasionally saw him step out to fetch ingredients or serve food. He had an almost meditative presence when he cooked. Every movement was slow and deliberate, as if he instinctively knew how much spice or salt to add without tasting it.

One day, when we were the only guests at the small restaurant, Ravi suddenly sat down at our table. "How long have you worked here?" Olof asked curiously.

"I came here when I was 16," Ravi said, glancing at Dilan and Amara. "I had no money and nowhere to stay. Dilan gave me a job, and Amara taught me everything I know about cooking. Now, it's my life."

Ravi quietly shared that he had a dream of opening his own restaurant one day. But he seemed in no rush. He was content here, and it was as if time moved more slowly in this place, as if his future was not something he needed to chase.

In the evenings, as the sun dipped below the horizon and painted the sky with hues of orange and purple, we often lingered at the restaurant long after finishing dinner. During those quiet moments, Dilan would sometimes join us, pulling up a chair and settling in as if we were old friends. He would share stories from his youth, his voice carrying the rhythm of the waves as he spoke about how the sea had always been woven into the fabric of his life.

One evening, after a particularly stunning sunset, we lingered at our table longer than usual. The air remained warm, but a gentle breeze from the sea swept across the beach, carrying with it the faint scent of salt and ocean. Dilan joined us, pulling up a chair and settling in as the twilight deepened.

"The sea has been a part of my life for as long as I can remember," he began, his gaze fixed on the horizon where the waves rolled in with a soothing rhythm. "My father was a fisherman, just like his father before him. Following in their footsteps was always meant to be my path." He paused, his fingers absently combing through his graying hair as he seemed lost in thought.

"The sea has given us so much," he continued after a reflective moment. "It's provided food, a livelihood, and the means to build this place." He gestured toward the bungalows and the restaurant surrounding us, a quiet pride in his voice. "But the sea can also take."

We sat in silence, sensing that Dilan was about to share something deeper, something close to his heart.

"I had a brother," Dilan said suddenly, his voice softer now, almost distant. "We were both young, maybe seven or eight years old. Our father used to take us out to sea sometimes when he went fishing. We couldn't wait to go with him, eager to prove ourselves, to be like him—strong and skilled fishermen."

He paused, lowering his gaze to the sand as though reliving the memory. "One day, the sea wasn't as calm as it seemed. My brother fell overboard." His voice dropped to a whisper. "Our parents did everything they could, but... the sea took him."

We sat in silence, motionless. The weight of his words hung in the air, so heavy it felt as if the sea itself had pulled back, leaving space for his sorrow to surface.

"After that," he continued, his voice steady but filled with emotion, "I came to understand something about the sea. It gives, but it also takes. Amara and I built this place with that understanding—that the sea is never something to take for granted." He lifted his eyes to meet mine, and the depth of his gaze was almost overwhelming. "That's why we pray for calm waters every day."

Amara stepped out from the kitchen then and joined him, placing her hand gently on his arm. Her presence mirrored his sadness but also his strength. "We love the sea," she said softly, her voice calm yet resolute. "But we've learned to respect it. It can give us everything, but it can also take away what we hold most dear."

That evening, we lingered at the table, talking with Dilan and Amara long into the night. They spoke about their lives and how, despite their loss, they had chosen to stay and build something beautiful by the sea. "We didn't want sorrow to define us," Dilan explained. "The sea has given us so much, and we wanted to create a place where people could experience its beauty—but always with respect."

During our week in Mirissa, we grew close to them. Dilan and Amara had built their little corner of paradise with love and resilience, creating a space that reflected their passion for hospitality and their deep, complex relationship with the sea. Ravi, their younger assistant, embodied hope for the future—a young man with big dreams who planned to one day create something of his own. For now, though, they were a team, and their restaurant felt like a second home.

Each day, one sight captivated us more than anything else: the local fishermen perched on their simple wooden stilts out in the water. They sat like statues, balanced on crossbeams tied to narrow poles, patiently fishing for hours. It was surreal—a serene, timeless tableau against the endless motion of the waves. Their quiet perseverance felt like an extension of the land itself, as natural as the swaying palms and the ever-changing ocean.

We ventured out on small excursions as well. One day, we visited a nearby fish market, where we watched fishermen haul in their catches straight from the sea. The market was alive with color and energy, a vibrant contrast to the subdued stillness of the stilt fishermen. It was fascinating to compare it to the fish markets back home in Gothenburg. On our way back, we stopped at roadside fruit stands and filled our bags with ripe mangoes and papayas. Their sweetness lingered on my tongue, a reminder of the abundance this place had to offer.

As we wound our way back to the bungalows that evening, the thought crossed my mind: time seemed to stand still here. It was a place that welcomed you, embraced you, and refused to let go. And I didn't want it to.

SEVEN

Chamali continued her tour of the house through the video call. "This part is newly built, and here's my room!" she said proudly, as the camera panned over a bright, simple interior. I observed the familiar details. Despite the changes, I could still see remnants of the old house beneath the new. It felt both strange and familiar, as if two eras were merging in the same place.

"What different lives we've led," I thought as I watched the screen. Chamali still lived at home when she wasn't called away for military duty, while I had just finished building my family's villa, had two children, and ran a consulting business within a large corporation. Our lives had taken such divergent paths, yet there was a connection between us that was undeniable.

"I'll show you the upstairs," Chamali continued, beginning to climb the narrow staircase. A familiar tightness gripped my stomach as I saw the unmistakable wooden stairs and the faint light streaming through the small windows. It was as if memories of my first

encounter with the house were slowly resurfacing — the room, the scent of damp wood, and the sound of rain drumming on the roof.

As the camera panned across the upper floor, the knot in my stomach tightened further. I recognized all too well how the upstairs looked. The clay roof tiles, the ones visible from inside the room, were still the same. "Do you remember your old room?" Chamali asked, laughing. Her laughter was as lighthearted as it had been back then, but it carried the weight of all the years that had passed.

"Yes, I remember," I replied, smiling, though with an inexplicable feeling of sadness. All the memories, both the bright and the dark, suddenly felt so close.

December 19, 2004
Mirissa, Sri Lanka

The Bob Marley lookalikes we had first met on that rainy night in their treehouse turned out to be so much more than we had imagined. They weren't just dreamers smoking under lanterns; they were also skilled surfers—and genuinely kind people. Their laid-back lifestyle, which had initially seemed so alien to us, began to grow on me.

For them, surfing wasn't just a hobby; it was a lifestyle, almost like a religion. Every day they went out to the ocean, unhurried and without stress. It wasn't about competing or showing off; it was about feeling one with the waves, about living in the moment. Though we had first assumed they just sat around in their hazy bubble, it turned out they took their surfing very seriously. Out on the water, their movements were precise and graceful, as if they could predict exactly what the wave would do before it even formed.

We quickly learned how much the ocean meant to them, and to our surprise, they offered to teach us how to surf. "It's something you just have to experience," said their leader, the guy with the longest dreadlocks and a perpetually calm, content smile.

The first lesson was slow and clumsy. Our attempts to master the small waves along the shore mostly ended in laughter and splashes as we toppled off the boards before even standing up properly. But the surf crew was patient, laughing with us as much as we laughed at ourselves. We soon realized that, for them, surfing was a way to meditate, a way to connect with nature and themselves. They treated the ocean with the same seriousness they did the waves.

It was my dad, who provided the most laughs. Always eager to challenge himself, surfing seemed to be a hurdle he just couldn't overcome. Despite all his attempts, careful instructions, and countless tries to balance on the board, he almost always ended up in the water with a giant splash. We stood on the beach clutching our sides with laughter as he lost his balance time and again. "I didn't think it would be this hard!" he shouted, floundering in the waves as they rushed around him.

The Bob Marley guys laughed too, but their laughter was warm and encouraging. They never judged him, continuing to offer tips and advice as if he were one of their own. "It's about feeling the wave, not fighting it," they repeated, and Dad nodded seriously, as if trying to absorb their wisdom.

But no matter how much advice he got, he kept falling off the board—turning his attempts into daily entertainment for all of us.

Still, there was something beautiful about it. We might not have been the best surfers, but we had fun, and every failure became a memory, every splash a laugh that brought us closer to each other and to the place we were in. As we laughed and struggled with the boards, it felt like we were becoming part of something bigger—a simple, natural joy that made us forget everything else for a while.

I felt their lifestyle, which had initially seemed so foreign, start to make more and more sense. There was an ease in the way they lived, a fluid freedom that made me want to let go of control and routines.

We also spent many afternoons on the beach with them. When surfing became too exhausting or the waves too challenging, we played beach volleyball under the blazing sun. The Bob Marley crew, with their sun-kissed bodies and muscular arms, moved with such ease and skill it was hard to believe they were the same people who lounged so lazily in their treehouses. Despite their laid-back vibe, they were incredibly talented, both at surfing and volleyball. They flew across the sand, leaping and spiking the ball with a precision that made Olof and me struggle to keep up.

We did our best to keep pace, but no matter how hard we tried, we could never quite match their level. They seemed almost one with the beach, as natural there as the sand beneath our feet. When we dropped the ball or missed a shot, they just laughed and patted us on the shoulders—always kind, always encouraging. There was no stress, no competition—just pure, simple joy. Every match became a game, and even when we lost, there was no frustration, only happiness.

After the matches, when we were all sweaty and covered in sand, they would head to their only shower—a simple, exposed stream of water that flowed down outside the treehouse, directly on the beach. The shower was so primitive it resembled a garden hose tied to a tree, but they didn't seem to care. They stood under the water with the ocean as their backdrop, letting it wash away the sand and sweat. We definitely saw more of them than we ever expected. The shower had no walls, and they didn't bother with discretion. They scrubbed themselves cheerfully, talking loudly and laughing, as if their bodies were just another part of the nature surrounding us. There was no embarrassment for them, nothing to hide. It was simply their way of life—simple, natural, and entirely carefree.

For us, coming from a more reserved and privacy-focused culture, it was a peculiar experience. Although I could never imagine showering stark naked on a beach surrounded by people, I started to understand their perspective. There was a freedom in the way they lived, a lightness. Their lives on the beach weren't about comfort or appearances but about being in the moment, enjoying every second. Slowly but surely, I began to adopt that lifestyle too.

Over the following days, I also started getting to know the other guests at the resort. Dilan and Amara's bungalows were simple yet charming, attracting travelers from all over the world—people looking for something peaceful and secluded, far away from the tourist trails. Soon, we began to feel like part of the little community forming there.

One of the families was from France. The father, Pierre, was a devoted surfer. He had a relaxed demeanor, and we often saw him out on the water, floating on his board while waiting for the perfect wave. His wife, Sophie, was an artist. Every morning, she would sit by the beach with her small easel, painting pictures of the ocean, the shore, and the towering palm trees swaying in the breeze. Their two young boys, both blond and bursting with energy, were constantly running up and down the shoreline, eager to explore everything nature had to offer.

One day, I sat next to Sophie as she painted. "It's a beautiful life we have here, isn't it?" she said in her soft French accent. She looked up from her easel and gazed at the ocean, where Pierre was just catching a wave. "We travel a lot for Pierre's surfing, but I must say, this is one of the most beautiful places I've ever been."

She showed me some of her paintings, and I was struck by how effortlessly she captured the ocean's depth and the shimmering sand with her simple, elegant brushstrokes. Each piece seemed to hold a quiet reverence for the sea, as though she had distilled its essence onto the canvas. "The sea is my greatest inspiration," she said, her voice calm and reflective. "It's always changing—just like life."

In another bungalow lived an older British woman named Margaret. Despite traveling alone, her lively energy and zest for life quickly made her a cherished part of our little group.

Margaret was no stranger to Sri Lanka—she had visited many times before and delighted in sharing tales of her adventures.

"There's something truly special about this place," she said one evening as we sat on the beach, watching the sun dip below the horizon. Her voice held a warmth that matched the glow of the setting sun. "I've traveled to so many corners of the world, but I always find my way back here. It's as if the sea is calling me home."

Margaret, an avid birdwatcher, would often set out early in the morning to explore the shoreline and nearby trees in search of the exotic birds native to the region. She carried a small, well-worn notebook where she meticulously documented every species she encountered, her neat handwriting filling the pages with names and observations. "Nature here never stops amazing me," she said, her face lighting up as she showed us the notebook. "Each bird feels like a new treasure waiting to be discovered."

EIGHT

Chamali finished the tour, and we laughed at the memories of the old room, when another voice suddenly emerged in the background. I instantly recognized the gentle, friendly tone of an older woman speaking in Sinhalese. Chamali turned around and smiled broadly at the camera.

"It's Mom," she said, motioning for the woman to come closer. "Sumudu, come say hello!" she called, and soon Sumudu appeared on screen, dressed in a colorful sarong and wearing her warm, welcoming smile. Her dark hair was streaked with gray, but her eyes still sparkled with the same kindness I remembered so well.

"Hello, hello!" Sumudu laughed in her slightly hesitant English, waving at the camera. She said something else in Sinhalese, and Chamali chuckled before translating, "Mom is asking how you're doing. She remembers you and your family very well."

"We're doing well, thank you," I replied softly, smiling warmly back at the screen. It felt like yesterday, but at the same time, like an

eternity ago. "I have my own family now," I added and called for my kids and husband, who were in another room. "Come and say hi!"

After a few seconds, my husband and children appeared behind me, a little shy but curious to see who I was talking to. "This is my husband and our two kids," I said proudly, brushing my hand over the children's hair. I introduced them as they politely waved at the screen. Sumudu smiled broadly and nodded approvingly.

Sumudu said something again in Sinhalese and laughed heartily. Chamali translated with a laugh, "Mom says you have a beautiful family and a handsome husband." Sumudu gave her daughter a teasing look and said something else in her native language, which made Chamali burst into laughter.

"Mom says I need to hurry up and find a husband and have kids now!" Chamali giggled, but there was a hint of playful self-awareness in her eyes. "She always teases me about not being married yet."

I smiled, amused by their familial dynamic. "Your time will come," I replied warmly. "You have your whole life ahead of you."

"I hope so," Chamali said, blushing slightly but still smiling. Sumudu added something more in Sinhalese, and Chamali translated with a laugh, "Mom says she's proud of me anyway, even if the military is my only companion!" We all laughed together, and I felt the warmth and closeness flow through the screen.

The mood lightened, and the conversation drifted into small talk about daily life, family, and future plans. I felt my heart swell with *an unexpected sense of reconciliation—despite all the years that had passed, there was still a deep connection between me and this Sri Lankan family. It felt like coming home, even from the other side of the world.*

December 22, 2004
Mirissa, Sri Lanka

One day, when Dilan thought we were ready for an adventure, he suggested we visit a snake farm located in the mountains—a place he had visited many times, as he knew the man who ran it. "It's a special place," he said with a faint smile. "Not for the faint-hearted, but I think you'll find it interesting."

Curiosity got the better of us, and we decided to make the trip up into the mountains. The journey took us through lush jungle, where the treetops stretched high into the sky and sunlight only occasionally reached the ground. The air grew cooler as we traveled, a welcome change from the coastal heat. The road wound its way through the dense greenery, and we felt ourselves being transported further from the calm of the beach and into another world.

When we arrived at the snake farm, we were met with a strange sight. Nestled in the jungle, surrounded by verdant trees and twisting vines, the farm itself looked worn, almost dilapidated. The building was simple, made of wood that seemed to have withstood decades of weather and time. At the entrance stood the owner, a wiry man with rough hands and deeply etched bite scars on his arms and neck—marks of a life lived close to dangerous animals.

"Welcome!" he called in a raspy but enthusiastic voice. He greeted us like old friends and beckoned us to follow him into the farm. Inside, it was almost like a museum of dangers. Small wooden boxes and birdcages filled with snakes, some moving slowly and others coiled, were everywhere. The air was thick with the smell of damp earth and reptiles. The snakes stared at us through the wire mesh with cold, inscrutable eyes.

"My father started this farm," he said proudly, pointing to an old, yellowed photograph hanging on one of the walls. The picture showed a sturdier version of the man in front of us, with the same rough hands and determined gaze. "He was one of the first in Sri Lanka to work on developing antivenom."

We listened as the man told us how his father had dedicated his life to studying snakes and their venom. "My father used to say that we are like the snakes themselves. We live side by side with danger, but with the right knowledge and respect, we can survive." He glanced around the room with a look that seemed to capture its entirety, and every cage appeared to remind him of his father.

He continued, "My father invented the antivenom many years ago, and it saved countless lives. He traveled around the country, selling it to hospitals and doctors, and he became a hero here in the mountains until tragedy struck."

"What happened?" Olof asked, his eyes wide with fascination for snakes.

"As life often is, it was ironically the snake that took him," the man replied with a faint smile, though sadness lingered behind it. "One night, during an experiment, he was bitten by a very venomous cobra. He was alone, and before he could reach his own antivenom... the snake claimed his life."

We stood there, silent and almost motionless, the weight of the story hanging in the air. The man's words echoed in our minds—a lifetime spent understanding and controlling a deadly danger, only to fall victim to the very threat he sought to combat.

Despite the loss, the son had continued his father's work. "We still have the antivenom," he said, gesturing to a shelf filled with small vials. "It's saved my life more than once. Snakes are not our enemies, but they're not our friends either. They do what they're made to do."

As we walked around, looking at the snakes, the man offered me the chance to hold a massive anaconda. Its cold, heavy body draped over my shoulders, and I could feel the faint movement of its muscles beneath its scales. I stood frozen, equal parts awe and fear, while Dad took a photo. "It's not dangerous," the man said with a wink. "It doesn't bite."

Despite his reassuring words, there was something unsettling about the experience. The snakes, with their silent, cold presence, served as a reminder that danger always lurked, even in the calmest moments. The old bite scars on the man's arms were a quiet testament to his life's work—to understand and survive in a world filled with both beauty and peril.

The mood in the taxi was slightly subdued as we slowly descended the winding jungle road. The trees stood close together, and the light from the setting sun filtered through the leaves in narrow beams. After visiting the snake farm, the jungle around us suddenly felt much more alive, as if we could now sense the raw power in every branch and every sound coming from the depths of the forest.

Suddenly, the taxi slowed down, snapping me out of my thoughts. The driver muttered something and came to a complete stop. Ahead of us, a tuk-tuk had stopped, and a small group of people stood by the roadside, gesturing animatedly and deep in conversation.

The taxi driver turned off the engine, opened his door, and stepped out with a deep breath. "I'll see what's going on," he said, walking toward the group ahead. We watched him as he motioned for us to come closer. Opening the doors, we stepped out and began to approach.

As we got closer, the driver met us halfway and, with a slight laugh, pointed ahead. "Come and look," he said. "But don't get too close."

We joined the others, cautiously moving forward, and there in the middle of the road lay a massive monitor lizard, stretched out like a living barricade that no one dared cross. It was so large it almost seemed unreal, its long body blending into the dark soil beneath it.

The group of locals was deep in discussion, speaking quickly in Sinhala, while an elderly man slowly shook his head. It was clear no one really knew what to do. The monitor lizard lay there, completely unbothered by the growing crowd gathering around it.

The taxi driver explained that monitors often moved slowly across jungle roads and could sometimes stop traffic for hours. "They're not dangerous as long as you keep your distance," he said. "But you must never get too close. They can be unpredictable and may become aggressive if they feel threatened."

"It's huge," Dad whispered. We kept a safe distance, just as the driver had advised. "It almost looks like a dinosaur," he added, studying the creature with a mix of fascination and respect.

Olof, who I would consider a true reptile nerd, knew much more about monitor lizards than the rest of us. He eagerly began explaining that monitors belong to the lizard family *Varanidae* and are found in many parts of the world, including Asia, Africa, and Australia. The species we were now facing was likely a Bengal monitor, according to Olof, one of the largest lizard species in Sri Lanka. These monitors can grow over two meters long and are primarily carnivorous, though they also eat fruit and insects.

"The Bengal monitor is known for its slow and majestic movements and its ability to defend itself quickly if threatened," Olof continued. "They have powerful claws and a strong tail, which they use both for defense and to climb trees or dig. Despite their size, they're often shy and prefer to avoid contact with humans, so seeing one like this is rare."

"Monitors are also excellent swimmers and are often seen near water sources. They're incredibly adaptable and can survive in both dry and humid environments. While they're not as dangerous as some other reptiles, caution is still necessary, especially if they feel cornered or threatened." Olof concluded his lecture and continued to observe the enormous lizard on the road with fascination.

The lizard remained motionless, seemingly indifferent to our presence. Its dark eyes blinked slowly, and it turned its large head slightly toward us, as if contemplating moving, but ultimately deciding to stay put. There was no rush, no urgency—only a profound stillness that seemed to encompass the entire scene.

The people around us began chatting and laughing softly, as if they understood there was nothing to do but wait. "It'll move when it's ready," the taxi driver said with a chuckle. "We just have to wait for it to decide."

We stood there, watching the monitor lizard, a symbol of nature's calm and unhurried pace. Nothing could force it to move, and no one dared come close enough to try. Here, nature had its own rules, and we were merely guests in its domain.

Minutes passed, and more people gathered, captivated by the sight of the massive lizard sprawled across the road. The driver explained that this kind of encounter was common in jungle areas. "They decide when we can move on," he said with a laugh. "There's nothing we can do about it."

We all waited, almost as if we were part of nature's rhythm, still and patient. The people around us seemed to accept that this was beyond their control. Time slowed down as we watched the monitor lizard blink slowly, unmoving in its spot on the road. Its majestic indifference to our presence made the scene feel almost sacred.

Suddenly, a loud honk echoed from further down the road, snapping everyone out of their quiet observation. A large bus approached from the opposite direction, its headlights flashing and its horn blaring again. The crowd stepped back as the monitor lizard slowly raised its head, clearly disturbed by the noise. The bus driver honked a third time, more insistently this time, and the lizard reluctantly began to move. Its massive body curved as it lazily dragged itself toward the vegetation at the side of the road, its gaze lingering on the bus as it edged closer.

"That driver is making a mistake," our taxi driver muttered beside us, a note of irritation in his voice. "You should never be in such a hurry that you anger nature."

We stood silently as the monitor lizard finally disappeared into the bushes. The bus rumbled past us, its horn sounding one last time, leaving a cloud of dust in its wake. The crowd began to disperse, but our driver stood still, watching the bus with a worried expression. He shook his head slowly.

"They think they can control everything with noise and speed," he said, looking at us with a mix of disappointment and concern. "But nature has its own moods. And when you rush it, it can strike back." He lit a cigarette and exhaled the smoke slowly. "You have to respect the jungle and its inhabitants. Never be in such a hurry that you make nature angry."

We got back into the taxi, but his words lingered in the air. His warning about nature striking back if not shown respect felt like an unspoken truth—something we should all consider, though I wasn't sure how.

As we continued our journey through the green jungle, the forest seemed quieter somehow. I could feel that we all shared the same sense of awe—that we had just witnessed a small glimpse of how nature ruled this world and how human impatience could sometimes disturb its delicate balance

NINE

I soon noticed that my children were becoming increasingly curious about the women on the other side of the screen. They were eager to talk but their English was still quite limited. I laughed at their attempts to ask Chamali and Sumudu questions and took on the role of interpreter to facilitate the conversation.

"Mom, ask if she has a pet," my youngest daughter said, casting a curious glance at the screen.

"Do you have any pets?" I translated to Chamali.

Chamali laughed and shook her head. "No, we don't have any pets. But we do have plenty of wildlife around here, monkeys and birds especially."

The children giggled, fascinated. "Wow, monkeys! Ask if they have monkeys living near their house!"

"Are there monkeys living near your house?" I continued, throwing an amused glance at the screen.

"Yes, sometimes they come very close," Chamali replied, pointing toward the window. "We have to be careful; they like to steal food."

I translated again, and the kids were thrilled, talking over one another. "Can we visit? Can we see the monkeys?"

I laughed and translated their eager questions to Chamali, who smiled and nodded. "Of course, you're always welcome. The monkeys are waiting."

Sumudu said something in Sinhala, and Chamali nodded happily. "Mom says you must visit soon," Chamali translated with a smile.

The knot in my stomach tightened again. My thoughts began to swirl. Could I really manage to go back? To step on a plane again, land in the same place, take in the smells, hear the sounds—it was one thing to talk over a screen, safe in my own home, but returning would be something entirely different.

I tried to shake off the feeling that was slowly growing inside me. It wasn't just the journey back to Sri Lanka—it was the act of facing it all again. All the memories, all the emotions I had long tried to suppress. Could I handle it? Could I face what happened, or would everything come crashing down again? But amidst this whirlwind of emotions, when I met Chamali's expectant gaze, I knew I couldn't say no.

"Yes, we'll come soon," I heard myself say with a smile that didn't quite reach my eyes. I tried to mask my hesitation from the children,

who now looked at me with curiosity, and from Chamali, who seemed genuinely happy about the promise.

The knot in my stomach grew tighter. "It will be fine," I tried to convince myself in my thoughts. I have to go back… for their sake, for my own.

December 24, 2004
Mirissa, Sri Lanka

Christmas Eve arrived, and even though we were far from the traditional Swedish Christmas with snow and chilly winds, there was something magical about celebrating Christmas on a paradise beach in Sri Lanka. There was a certain charm in the soft, warm breeze, the gentle murmur of the ocean, and the swaying palms that made everything feel different yet just as special as back home. The sun shone in a way that felt almost sacred that day, as if it, too, wanted to give us a Christmas gift.

Early on Christmas morning, just when we thought all the bungalows were full, a rattling taxi pulled up in front of the small resort. Out stepped a Swedish family, and we exchanged surprised glances as we saw that they had two children about the same age as Olof and me. The mother, Agneta, smiled broadly and called out, "Merry Christmas!" as she got out of the taxi. The father, Erik, looked a bit more tired from the long journey, but he greeted us cheerfully when we met.

Agneta and Erik, like our parents, had decided to escape the Swedish winter and spend an unconventional Christmas in

Sri Lanka. Their daughter, Sofia, was my age, and we clicked instantly. She had long, blonde hair and wore a floral dress that fluttered in the warm wind. Her brother, Emil, was a bit older than Olof and slightly quieter, but I could tell Olof quickly found a friend in him.

Now all the bungalows were full, and it felt as though the resort had truly come to life. Despite coming from different parts of the world, we shared a camaraderie that made Christmas Eve feel special and intimate. It was a sense of being there to celebrate together, even if we were strangers to one another.

By lunchtime, after lounging for a while in our hammocks, we decided to go on a little adventure. Dilan had previously mentioned a small hill just behind the resort, and our curiosity got the better of us. Together with the Swedish family, we began our small expedition. It wasn't a massive hill, but for us, it felt like a real adventure. We climbed over rocks and through undergrowth, listened to the sounds of the jungle, and laughed at our clumsy attempts to navigate the uneven terrain.

Sofia and I led the way, joking about being real explorers, while Olof and Emil tried to impress us by climbing the highest rocks they could find. With every step we took higher, it felt as though we were moving further away from the world, away from stress and expectations. It was just us, nature, and the quiet bond forming between us.

When we reached the top of the small hill, a breathtaking view of the endless blue horizon unfolded before us. Below, the beach stretched like a thin white ribbon along the turquoise water, and we could see the bungalows as tiny dots along the coastline. We sat in silence for a while, taking in the view and savoring the feeling of being on top of the world, even if only for a moment.

Later in the afternoon, we returned to the bungalows, pleasantly tired yet content from our day's adventures. The air seemed to hum with a quiet sense of anticipation, as though we all sensed that the evening would be one to remember. Understanding that Swedes traditionally celebrate Christmas Eve rather than Christmas Day, Dilan and Amara had thoughtfully planned something special in our honor.

As the sun began its descent, painting the sky in soft hues of pink and orange, the preparations for a grand feast were well underway. Dilan and Amara had gathered fresh clams from the nearby waters, which they grilled over an open fire. The aroma of the seafood, seasoned and sizzling on the flames, mingled with the salty ocean breeze, making our mouths water. Bottles of Singha, the local Sri Lankan beer, were carefully placed on the tables, their chilled surfaces glistening in the fading sunlight.

The tables were set up directly on the beach, just a few meters from the water. There was no Christmas tree, no gifts, and no carols, yet the atmosphere was as warm and filled with togetherness as any Christmas back home in Sweden. Dilan and Amara had gone out of their way to make the evening special for us, and it truly felt as though we were celebrating something grand and meaningful together, despite being so far from our usual traditions.

After dinner, we gathered around a small bonfire on the beach. There was something almost magical about sitting there in the glow of the flames, with the sound of waves lapping at the shore and the stars sparkling above us. We talked about our homes, our journeys, and all the strange and beautiful things we had seen during our time in Sri Lanka.

Dilan shared stories about how he and Amara had built their little resort piece by piece and how their dream was to create a place where people from all over the world could come and find peace and tranquility. It was clear that they loved the life they had built, and their passion was contagious to everyone around them.

We all enjoyed the serene atmosphere of the evening. There was an effortless calm in the air, a feeling that everything was exactly as it should be. No stress, no demands—just a simple and beautiful Christmas Eve on a beach far away from everything.

That night, between Christmas Eve and Christmas Day, I felt completely at ease. My thoughts barely touched on what awaited me at home or what the next day would bring. It was as if time had stopped, and all that mattered was the present moment—being on the beach with my new friends and feeling the warm ocean breeze sweeping over us.

But when night fell, my sleep was restless. Despite the calm and joyful mood during our Christmas dinner and the peaceful silence on the beach, something gnawed at me. Perhaps it was all the stories about snakes and the slow, unyielding presence of the monitor lizard the day before that had lodged themselves in my mind. I didn't know why, but when I finally fell asleep, my night was filled with dreams—and a peculiar nightmare took hold of me.

Suddenly, I was back in the mountains we had visited the day before. The humid jungle wrapped around me like a living entity, and the heat radiating from the ground seeped into my skin. The world felt unnervingly still, as if nature itself had paused to hold its breath. Then, without warning, everything shifted. The animals, which had been almost silent and unseen, began to behave erratically. At first, it was just faint noises—the soft rustle of leaves and distant, low growls. But those subtle sounds quickly swelled into a deafening symphony of chaos. Birds erupted from the treetops, their piercing cries slicing through the dense, heavy air, and the ground beneath my feet started to tremble, as though something immense and unseen had been awakened.

I looked around, and suddenly, we were no longer alone. Animals seemed to come from all directions—snakes, monitor lizards, monkeys, even small insects—all moving quickly and desperately. It was as if the jungle itself had gone mad. I could hear their panic in the loud cries, and it was as though all of nature was trying to warn me of something. I wanted to run, but my legs felt heavy, stuck as if in quicksand.

Then, out of nowhere, a deep rumbling sound filled the air. The ground beneath my feet began to shake violently, and I saw the jungle plants, once motionless, swaying wildly. Suddenly, I saw it—a massive wave of glowing lava rolling through the jungle like a scorching, pulsating river. It was a wave that couldn't be stopped, consuming everything in its path.

Panic gripped me. "We have to climb! We have to get up!" I screamed, but my words were drowned out by the deafening roar of the approaching lava. I watched as the lava licked the ground, turning tree trunks to ash and splitting stones with its intense heat. The warmth was so intense that it felt like it was sucking the air out of my lungs.

We ran—me, Olof, Mom, and Dad—and suddenly, there were large boulders in front of us. We began to climb, desperate to escape the boiling lava that continued to advance. I could feel the stone under my hands growing hotter with each passing second, and it felt as though the lava would reach us at any moment. The animals, which had seemed frenzied before, now climbed alongside us on the rocks, as if we were all fighting for the same thing—to survive.

But the lava came closer. It devoured everything in its path, and it was as if the entire jungle melted away beneath us. I felt trapped, with nowhere to go, as the lava threatened to drag us into its flaming depths. Sweat poured down my face, and I could feel my body freezing in fear.

Suddenly, I woke up, gasping for breath, my heart pounding hard in my chest. The darkness in the room enveloped me, and it took a few seconds before I realized I had only been dreaming. But the feeling of danger lingered. It was as if nature had tried to tell me something in the dream, a warning that something big was about to happen.

I lay there for a long time, staring out the window, trying to shake off the strange feeling. Outside, I could hear the muffled sound of waves rolling onto the shore, and everything was calm and peaceful. I lay there, listening to the sound of the waves for a long time before I finally drifted back to sleep.

TEN

When the call ended, I sat with the phone in my hand for a while. The screen was dark now, and the silence in the room felt heavy after the lively voices and laughter that had just filled the house. Outside the window, the sound of rain drummed against the glass, and a sudden feeling of emptiness swept over me. It was as if something large and weighty had been dragged out of a dark corner of my memory, leaving me sitting there with all the emotions I had suppressed for so many years. Would I really dare to go back? Could I handle it?

The house around me was quiet now. The children were asleep after my husband had put them to bed, and I knew he would soon return to check on me after the call. I thought back to my time in Sri Lanka, to our unexpected friendship with the family there, to everything we had shared. I thought about the surfers, the beach, the simple yet beautiful existence in paradise before the catastrophe struck. I thought about Dilan and Amara and how they had fought to build their paradise.

But most of all, I thought about Chamali. How life had taken us in such different directions, how we had once shared an intensely chaotic time together and then disappeared from each other's lives. And now, after all these years, we had found our way back to each other, even if it was just through a screen. Was it fate that brought us together again? Or was it something else—a lingering guilt or an unresolved chapter I had never truly been able to let go of?

I got up and walked slowly through the living room, where toys were scattered across the floor. The children's small voices and laughter from earlier in the day echoed in my memory. I moved to the window and looked out at the Swedish autumn landscape—rain fell heavily, and the trees' leaves had started turning yellow and red. Sweden. So different from Sri Lanka. Here was everything I knew, everything I had built—my family, my home, my job. But there was also something else, a part of me that had always stayed in the past, in those chaotic days on the other side of the world.

My husband entered the room and stood by my side. "How did it go?" he asked, with that warm look that always calmed me.

I shook my head, unsure how to answer. "It went well. It was... overwhelming."

"Do you think you'll go there?" He asked the question carefully, but with a hint of knowing what my answer might be.

I sighed deeply. "I don't know. I promised I would. But... I don't know if I can."

We stood in silence for a while, looking out into the darkness together. The rain kept tapping against the window, and my thoughts swirled like the leaves outside. I was afraid of what a return would mean. Would I face them as the person I am today or as the person I was back then? Would the stress, fear, sorrow, and shame return the moment I stepped back there?

December 25, 2004
Mirissa, Sri Lanka

Christmas Day was a day of unhurried simplicity. After a shared breakfast on the beach, with the sun already rising high in the sky, we embraced a slower pace. The warmth was soothing, and the sea, with its gently rolling waves, seemed to beckon us. Time itself felt as though it had softened, allowing us to bask in a shared sense of peace and freedom.

We started the day with a swim in the crystal-clear water, cooling our sun-warmed bodies. The gentle waves were perfect for beginners like us to continue practicing surfing. Pierre, the French surfer, helped us and the other guests improve our techniques. His infectious enthusiasm and patience made us all feel like pros, even when our attempts to stand on the boards often ended with us tumbling into the water amidst laughter.

After surfing, we gathered on the beach for a friendly game of beach volleyball. Everyone joined in—adults and kids alike—and it was equal parts competition and play. We laughed loudly when the ball flew too far, and though the rules weren't always followed to the letter, the atmosphere was full of joy and camaraderie. Even Ravi, the chef, joined in, proving to be a skilled player and cheering us on as we struggled to keep the ball in play.

The other guests, including the Swedish family and the older British woman Margaret, watched from the shade of a palm tree, applauding every time someone scored. It became a day filled with play, laughter, and pure joy. Though far from home, we felt surrounded by friends, and the beach became our shared playground.

As the afternoon turned to evening, the beach slowly emptied. We sat down to rest after all the activity, and the sky shifted from blue to shades of orange, pink, and purple. The warm air was filled with the sound of waves and the soft voices of other guests retreating to their bungalows.

That evening, Dilan and Amara's two children joined us. Their son and daughter, both in their mid-20s, had traveled from Colombo to spend Christmas Day with their parents. Having grown up on this beach, it was clear that, despite their lives in the bustling city, the rhythm of the sea and this place remained a deep part of who they were.

"It always feels like coming home when we're here," their daughter said, her warm smile a reflection of her mother's. She gazed out at the sea, a hint of nostalgia in her eyes. "Nothing in the city compares to this."

That evening, we all gathered on the beach. Tables and chairs were arranged in a circle, and the light came from small lanterns hanging in the trees and the stars twinkling above. The children played in the sand while the adults talked and laughed over dinner. Pierre and Sophie shared stories of their travels, Margaret entertained us with tales of her past adventures, and the Swedish family described their Christmas traditions back home.

Dilan and Amara moved among us, serving food and making sure we had everything we needed. There was something about their presence that felt integral to the place itself—their calmness, their warmth. They weren't just the owners of the small resort; they were the soul of the entire experience.

As the evening progressed, we all sank deeper into a sense of peace and contentment. It was as if the world beyond no longer existed, as if time had stopped. The sound of the waves, the soft murmur of conversations, and the warm light of the lanterns created an atmosphere that we would all carry with us forever.

And though we were on a tropical island, far from the twinkling lights of Christmas trees and snow-covered streets, it felt like one of the most memorable Christmases we had ever experienced. We celebrated together, as a colorful group of strangers who had transformed into friends, united by the sense of community on this little stretch of coastline.

We talked about our different Christmas traditions, and Dilan and Amara's children shared stories from their childhood on the beach—about playing in the sand and learning to swim in the small coves.

"We loved playing beach volleyball here as kids," their son said, glancing at the volleyball net that still stood. "It looks like you're keeping the tradition alive."

The night gently descended over the beach, casting a soft veil of twilight across the shore. A deep sense of togetherness settled among us, as natural and steady as the waves lapping at the sand. We lingered there for hours, talking and laughing, the passing time unnoticed and unimportant. It felt as though the sea itself had cast a spell of tranquility, wrapping us all in a shared moment of pure serenity.

ELEVEN

I sat in the sheepskin armchair I had inherited from my grandmother a few years earlier. Wrapped in a blanket, with a mug of coffee in my hands, I stared into the darkness outside the window. It was 4 a.m., and the cold sweat from my dreams still clung to my skin—a sticky reminder of something unfinished, something demanding my attention.

I tried to take a deep breath, letting the aroma of coffee surround me, but my heart was still pounding hard against my chest. My thoughts drifted back to the evening before, to the conversation with Chamali, which had opened a box of memories I had long avoided.

My gaze traced the familiar contours of the house—the room with the large windows I had insisted on, the high ceilings, and the open spaces. I had designed it all, encouraged by my husband. Together with family and close friends, we had poured endless time and effort into turning what was once just a sketch on paper into a reality.

We had built our home together, a project filled with laughter, frustration, sweat, and tears, and I often thought back to those who marveled at my courage to take on something so big and uncertain. How did I dare dive into projects like these?

*A faint sigh escaped my lips. *"I've been given a second chance to try everything,"* I thought, catching my reflection in the glass—a silhouette against the dark landscape. And I had set out to do just that. I had gone through life with the attitude that nothing was impossible. Bold, some said, and cocky, according to many.*

Frankly, I didn't care much what people thought. I had survived, made it back to a place where life could be rebuilt, and I was determined to fight for it. Perhaps that's why I dared to take on so much—because I had already seen the worst, felt death's presence, and come out the other side. I had told myself not to waste a second and to try everything. And everything, I truly had tried.

Oddly enough, I had always been fearless when it came to the projects and adventures I pursued. I dared to do things others deemed reckless—I had leaped off waterfalls and jumped out of planes, balanced on cliff edges, paddled near crocodiles, snorkeled with sharks, and ventured into stormy seas. I embraced challenges head-on, constantly testing the limits.

Once, I even managed to provoke half of Sweden's carpenters when I appeared on TV, boldly declaring, "How hard can it be?" as I designed and built my own house—despite having no formal training.

Whether in my personal life or at work, I threw myself into everything with unrelenting energy. Reckless? Perhaps. But those risks made me feel truly alive. I savored every moment, every second.

Nothing ever held me back! But now, for the first time, I felt myself beginning to falter. It was as though I was being drawn into a black hole all over again.

December 26, 2004
Matara, Sri Lanka

On December 26th, we were ready to leave Mirissa. We had planned to catch an early bus to Matara and then continue along Sri Lanka's east coast. We wanted to explore more of the country, to see the places we had heard so much about. But we also knew that some areas were off-limits. Traveling too far north was not an option. The conflict with the Tamil Tigers—a struggle that had shaped Sri Lanka for decades—still left its mark on the country. For us, it was a limitation, but for the people we met, it was an ongoing reality, something they had adapted their lives around for years.

I remember how my father explained the conflict as we packed our backpacks earlier that morning. He told us how the tensions dated back to the colonial era in the 19th century, when the British ruled and granted special privileges to the Tamils, a minority in Sri Lanka. Access to the best education, public sector jobs, and other advantages placed the Tamils in a position that the Sinhalese majority would come to resent deeply. After Sri Lanka gained independence from Britain in 1948, these historical grievances laid the groundwork for conflict. The Sinhalese majority began implementing laws and reforms that isolated the Tamils, excluding them from education and opportunities, which only fueled greater anger and frustration.

I tried to grasp the magnitude of what my father was describing—that these tensions had lasted so long that Tamil politicians eventually began demanding a separate state. The conflict had a name, and a movement had emerged to fight for it: the Tamil Tigers. Officially called the LTTE, the movement was founded in 1976 and fought for an independent Tamil state they called Tamil Eelam. It was led by Velupillai Prabhakaran, a man who quickly gained infamy not just in Sri Lanka but worldwide.

My father explained how the Tamil Tigers used guerrilla warfare and other brutal tactics to fight the government. Suicide bombings, political assassinations, child soldiers—their violence knew no bounds, and their control extended over large areas of northern and eastern Sri Lanka. Regions like the Jaffna Peninsula became their strongholds, and they established an entirely parallel society there—with schools, hospitals, and their own judicial system.

As we approached Matara on the bus, I also recalled how my father mentioned the 2002 peace agreement, brokered by Norway, that had never truly taken hold. The ceasefire had been broken multiple times, and the conflict had worsened due to a split within the Tamil Tigers. A senior commander had defected, taking a significant portion of the eastern forces with him. This split had weakened the movement but also made the situation even more precarious for those living in the affected areas.

The closer we got to Matara, the more I felt the weight of the country's history. My father didn't say much more, but the serious expression on his face spoke volumes. This was a country where conflicts still simmered beneath the surface, despite every effort toward peace and reconciliation. We were travelers, free to move between places, but there were parts of Sri Lanka that we—and many others—would never be able to reach.

The bus was overcrowded—apparently, there was a major holiday in Matara that day, and many people were traveling into the city. We squeezed in among cages of chickens and other passengers. The traffic was chaotic, and it felt as if we were part of a frenzied flow of people and vehicles, all trying to reach their destinations.

Amid the bustling crowd, I saw an elderly woman attempting to cross the road. Suddenly, a motorcycle sped toward her and struck her. Everything seemed to pause for a moment. People gathered around her, and although she appeared to be okay, it was a chilling reminder of how quickly everything could change.

When we arrived at the bus station in Matara, we had some time to spare. The station was built on pillars, which gave the entire area an elevated feeling above ground level. Buses pulled into a large, open platform on the ground floor, while above, up a flight of stairs, there were shops and small stalls selling everything from clothes to fruit and drinks. A large tiled roof covered the platform and the shops, creating a sense of a self-contained world, separate from the traffic and chaos below.

On the upper level, the steady sea breeze brought a refreshing coolness. A walkway encircled the entire building, offering sweeping views of the surroundings. As we ascended, we gazed out toward the ocean. There, in the distance, stood an island with a striking temple that shimmered like gold under the sunlight. A narrow causeway seemed to rise from the sea, connecting the island to the shore.

"That's something we should explore," I said.

"That'll have to be another time," my father replied. "Even though we have time, we'll never make it there and back before our bus departs."

We decided to find our bus instead. Eventually, we located the right one and took seats at the very back. We had plenty of time before the 9:30 departure. The large station clock read 9:00. The air inside the bus was heavy and humid, even with the small ventilation windows open. We sat close together, waiting for the journey to begin.

There was constant motion around us at the station. People came and went, either continuing their journeys or arriving and heading off into the busy streets and sidewalks. There was a muted hum in the air, like that of a small-town market, but with a relaxed, friendly vibe. People chatted and called out to one another, and the easygoing energy was infectious. But after a while, we noticed that the atmosphere outside was shifting.

The conversations around us grew louder, with people gesturing animatedly and moving briskly between the buses.

Some appeared anxious, while others stood motionless, staring toward the sea as though anticipating something. Our bus remained still amidst the growing commotion. Through the windows, we watched as people began to jog between vehicles, speaking urgently in Sinhala. There was a palpable tension in the air, an unease we couldn't fully grasp.

My mother, sitting in the seat in front of me, glanced out the window and sighed deeply. When some men began raising their voices and shouting to each other outside, she turned toward us with a concerned look. "It's probably a drug raid," she said, sounding almost intrigued. "Things like this happen sometimes—I've read about it." She explained how Sri Lanka had strict drug laws and that the police often conducted searches and raids, especially at stations and other busy places.

During our trip, we had all heard about the harsh penalties for drug-related crimes in the country. Signs at the airport warned of prison sentences and even the death penalty for smuggling, and we knew the police could search both passengers and luggage in their hunt for illegal substances.

We looked out the window, trying to understand what was happening. Small groups began to gather here and there, and a few uniformed men stood by the side of the road, engaged in serious discussions. It was clear that something had changed. The atmosphere grew increasingly tense, and more and more people started running between the buses. Someone called out to another, and soon the voices rose to a murmur. We heard shouts in Sinhala that we couldn't understand, but it was obvious that something was worrying the crowd.

It felt as if everyone knew something was about to happen, yet no one seemed to know exactly what or why. "What on earth is going on?" my mom said, twisting in her seat to get a better view through the window. Her eyes scanned the crowd outside, confused and searching for an answer. The uniformed men were trying to control the situation, but they themselves seemed uncertain.

Suddenly, the shouting intensified, piercing the air with urgency. When the policemen began blowing their whistles and sprinting toward the city, the panic truly set in. It was as if an unseen alarm had been triggered, unleashing chaos. People started screaming, their movements frantic as they raced away from the beach and toward the city.

Olof, seated beside me, turned toward the large rear window of the bus. His eyes narrowed as he stared at the distant sea. With a quiet, almost detached tone, he muttered, "I think a wave is coming."

TWELVE

I stared down into my coffee mug, watching the steam rise in thin, swirling tendrils. My thoughts drifted back to Sri Lanka. Though two decades had passed since that day, some feelings remained just as raw. What struck me now, so early in the morning, was the deep sense of injustice I had carried with me ever since. My family and I—we were able to leave it all behind, to return to the safety of Sweden, leaving behind the devastation and sorrow without having to remain in a country torn apart by loss and need. I couldn't imagine how hard it must have been for those who had no choice but to stay. The saltwater that had destroyed so much, the division in the country exacerbated by people's desperate fight to survive. Our passports and money were our tickets home, but for most of those we left behind, there was no "home" left.

The guilt over my own survival has gnawed at me for so long, a guilt that sometimes feels unbearable. I thought of Ruwan and his family, who opened their home to us, who took us into their lives amidst all the destruction. They stayed behind while we returned to warmth and abundance. I remembered the other children's eyes, how they simply accepted everything happening around them, as if catastrophe was just another part of life. That day when we said goodbye—I didn't know then that I would carry them with me forever.

Building my house, creating my life—was that my way of trying to tip the scales, to make something meaningful out of the years I was given? Is that why I've always fought so hard, to prove—perhaps to myself, perhaps to some higher power—that I deserved this second chance, a chance so many others never got?

December 26, 2004
Matara, Sri Lanka

A mother grabbed her two small children by the hands and rushed out of the bus, and soon others followed her lead.

Panic surged within me. "What do we do?" I asked, my voice trembling as I watched more and more people flee the bus.

From his seat at the back, Dad shouted, "Stay on the bus! Whatever you do, stay here and hold on!"

We obeyed him. Olof and I gripped the seats in front of us with our sweaty hands, trying to stay calm. But outside the bus, the world began to fall apart. A young man further up suddenly jumped out through the door, just seconds before it happened.

The first wave hit with a force I didn't think was possible. The water came in like an unrelenting monster, and the bus was tossed around like a toy. A loud crash echoed as the bus was slammed against one of the pillars holding up the upper level of the bus station. Everything shook, windows shattered, and we were flung back and forth, but we held on as tightly as we could.

I saw a boy about my age, standing in the aisle with nowhere to go, hurled toward the front windshield of the bus with such force that he collapsed to the floor. Blood streaked his face as he struggled to get up, his expression a mix of shock and terror. For a fleeting moment, our eyes met, but before I could process what was happening, I saw him leap out through the front door. He had no chance.

Outside, the wave grew even larger and stronger, destroying everything in its path. The bus, now wedged between the station's roof and one of the pillars, no longer moved, but the panic I felt was raw and sharp. What was happening? Were we about to die?

"We need to get up!" Dad yelled as the wave retreated slightly. He had climbed out through the door and now stood with one foot on a railing outside, wedging the other into one of the small open ventilation windows of the bus. The bus was an old, tall model with tiny windows that could be opened, and Olof managed to climb through, using Dad as a makeshift ladder. Dad pushed him onto the roof. It was high, but Olof made it up quickly. When I tried to follow, I couldn't reach.

"I can't do it!" I screamed in panic. "I can't!"

Dad's voice was desperate as he shouted back, "You have to do this!" He gave me a shove upward while Mom tossed me the small backpack containing all our money, passports, and the camera. I strapped it on and tried again.

Olof, now on the roof, screamed down, his voice panicked: "Hurry! Another wave is coming!"

He grabbed my hand and pulled with all his strength. Just as I managed to scramble onto the roof, the next wave hit, larger and more powerful than the first. Even though the bus station was elevated above the water, the destruction was immense.

Olof and I clung to the roof as the world around us fell apart. It felt like everything was shattering, like this was the end of everything we'd ever known. Dad was nowhere to be seen. He hadn't made it up. Mom had been left inside the bus, but now the water reached all the way up to the roof. If she was still there, she had no air left.

Lying there on the roof, I couldn't help but think: What have I done? Was it my fault that Mom and Dad were gone now? If I'd been faster getting onto the roof, could they have climbed up too? Were they dead? Could the bodies I occasionally glimpsed in the water be theirs?

I didn't think about it at the time, but looking back, I realize that my brain somehow shut down. Everything around me was chaos—waves tearing through cars and people, my brother screaming for Mom and Dad, and the water swallowing everything we knew. Yet despite the physical destruction, I remember a strange silence. It was as if the world around me had lost its voice, trapping me in a bubble of quiet.

At that moment, everything else faded away, and my mind fixed on one thing: my brother. His screams pierced through the chaos, cutting through the surrounding noise as though the world had gone silent except for him. He was calling for our parents, but they were nowhere in sight. All we could see was water—endless, overpowering, erasing the line between land and sea. Water and destruction—an all-encompassing force, drowning out every other sound.

THIRTEEN

I'm still sitting in the living room, holding the empty coffee cup in my hands, staring out through the large windows. The sun is starting to rise, but the rest of the family is still asleep. The soft morning light slowly spreads across the room, but my thoughts are already deeply rooted in another time, another place.

The memory of that day in Sri Lanka is like a film without sound, a silent, vivid sequence of images that I carry with me always.

I remember how I felt then — the paralyzing fear, the uncertainty. The images are so vivid: the waves surging in and out, people struggling around me, the makeshift safety of the bus roof. Yet somehow, my body had turned off the sound, as if I were watching everything from outside myself. I saw everything, but I heard nothing except my brother's voice. It was the only sound in that chaotic, muted landscape.

Later, when people asked me what it sounded like that day — if I remembered the roar of the waves or the cries of the people — I realized I couldn't describe it. I saw everything in detail, but I heard nothing except my brother's screams. When I tried to explain it to others, it was like narrating a silent film, one where I merely reacted without fully experiencing the reality. I could see all those scenes, but with a strange detachment—as if my mind had shut down parts of the experience to protect me.

The only thing that broke through was my brother's desperate voice. It was his voice that gave me the strength to hold on, to fight. His voice was like a lifeline, my anchor in a world full of visual chaos yet eerily silent. Perhaps that was exactly what I needed—to focus on his voice and block out everything else so I could survive.

They say the brain enters a survival mode when faced with extreme stress—a defense mechanism that shuts down certain senses so we can endure the unendurable. Perhaps that's exactly what happened to me. What remained when I came out on the other side was his voice, and that was enough to remind me what kept me alive, what I was fighting for.

Now, as I look back, I realize I can never fully recreate that day. I can see the images and remember his voice, but everything else is shrouded in a strange silence. And maybe that's how it has to be. Perhaps it was my way of surviving, my way of moving forward despite it all.

December 26, 2004
Matara, Sri Lanka

Eventually, I heard another voice besides my brother's desperate screams. It was a man standing on the upper level of the bus station, his voice cutting through the chaos. "Try to climb up!" he shouted, gesturing for us to come. I looked at Olof and told him to stand on my back to reach the man, but Olof shook his head, panic written all over his face.

"No! We have to find Mom and Dad!" he yelled back, and I felt the same anxiety welling up inside me. The wave had just started to recede, and both of us scanned the scene below, our eyes frantically searching through the debris and overturned buses. As the water began to pull back, shapes emerged. Among the wreckage and bodies being carried away by the current, we saw people—people clinging desperately to poles, gates, fences, and anything they could grasp. And then, amidst the chaos, we saw someone we recognized.

I have never felt such an overwhelming sense of relief as when I saw my dad. He was clinging to a pole, and another man, equally exhausted, was hanging onto him for support. Dad looked like he was on his last reserves of strength, his face twisted with exertion and pain. As the wave pulled back slightly, he got a brief moment of reprieve—a fleeting chance to catch his breath.

"Dad!" we screamed in unison, our voices echoing across the devastated landscape. Just then, as if by some miracle, we saw Mom stumble out of the bus. Her body was soaked, and she was coughing and spitting up water as she tried to regain her balance. Draped over her shoulders were our backpacks, hanging heavily behind her. Mom! They were alive! Both of them! Our beloved parents! A wave of relief washed over me. They were truly alive!

I must have been in some kind of shock because my next impulse was so absurd it didn't even feel real. I had this sudden idea that we needed evidence of what was happening, and I pulled out the camera. "Should I take a picture, Dad?" I asked, as if this were an ordinary day. Dad, struggling to stay upright, barely looked up when he replied, "Yes, take pictures of everything."

I raised the camera and started taking photos from the roof of the bus. It felt like we were in an entirely different world. Just minutes earlier, everything had been normal, but now the landscape was transformed into something resembling a war zone. Houses were in ruins, windows shattered, and buses lay scattered like discarded toys. Water and debris were strewn across the station, and people were struggling to regain their footing after the violent wave.

Amidst the chaos, I noticed a young man running with his wife close behind. Both were screaming frantically in Sinhala. The man was carrying an infant in his arms, and I saw that the child's body hung limp and lifeless. They were desperate, their cries piercing through the devastation as others rushed toward them, equally distraught. I didn't know then that this image would haunt my nightmares for years to come—their screams, their despair—it stayed with me.

Suddenly, the camera felt like a heavy, inappropriate object in my hands. It felt wrong to be taking pictures, capturing the suffering of others. Shame washed over me, and I quickly tucked the camera away. How could I even think about taking photos amidst such chaos?

My dazed state was interrupted by the same man who had called to us earlier from the upper level. "More waves! More waves! Hurry!" he yelled, and this time there was no hesitation. Olof and I quickly jumped off the roof of the bus, our backpacks heavy and soaked as we slung them over our shoulders. We ran as fast as we could toward the staircase leading to the upper level.

The scene at the staircase was chaotic. People were shoving and pushing, desperate to climb higher and find safety. An elderly woman stumbled in front of us, and I grabbed her arm just in time to stop her from falling. I helped her to her feet, and we continued fighting our way through the crowded stairwell. Eventually, we made it to the upper level and stopped to catch our breath. From the elevated position, we could see the full extent of the destruction stretching far across the city.

And then the next wave came.

It looked almost unreal as it surged forward. The water rushed in, destroying what little remained standing. Even though so much was already ruined, the wave continued its devastating path through the heart of the city. We saw people fighting for their lives, while others simply gave up and were swept away by the torrents. I saw an old man trying to climb onto a wall with the help of two younger men. But their efforts were futile. When the wave struck, the wall collapsed, and all three were carried away by the floodwaters.

We stood frozen, paralyzed by the sheer devastation unfolding around us. Dad, who always seemed to have a plan, now looked confused. He turned to a woman next to us and asked, "Has a dam broken? What's happening?" The woman, who seemed to be in shock herself, shouted back, "Yes, it's a dam!" No one really knew what had happened, only that something terrible and inexplicable had struck us all. The shock made it hard to think clearly, and everyone was speculating.

At the same time, we saw more people climbing onto the roof of the bus station, and we began discussing whether we should try to climb even higher. Would the station hold against more waves? Were we safe here, or would we need to flee to an even higher place?

As the third wave began to recede, we heard a whistle. Further down the street, a policeman was shouting for everyone to evacuate. "Run now!" Dad yelled, and we started running as fast as we could. We ran with the crowd, through the debris, jumping over bicycles and climbing over piles of bricks.

We passed people running in the opposite direction, desperate to find their loved ones. "Go home!" they shouted at us. But how could we possibly leave? Everything seemed broken and destroyed.

FOURTEEN

I hear my husband stirring, awake and moving about. He's in the bathroom, following the same morning routine he does every day. Even though his meticulousness sometimes frustrates me, there's a quiet comfort in hearing those familiar sounds. I can picture him clearly—carefully washing his face, behind his ears, even his nose—every step part of his practiced ritual.

As my thoughts drift, another image surfaces—one I've tried to bury, but it refuses to stay hidden. It's the image of the infant, cradled limply in its parents' arms. Its stillness haunts me, a stark and unshakable memory from those days in Sri Lanka.

In my dreams, that moment returns, vivid and relentless. I see the parents' faces twisted with grief, hear their anguished cries, and feel the icy grip of my own paralysis. I was so young then, far too young to comprehend fully what I was witnessing. Yet, the weight of the child's fate struck me with the force of a blade.

After we returned home, the nightmares came often. Whenever I closed my eyes, the child's face would appear, an unwelcome ghost in my sleep. I would wake up screaming, overcome by the helplessness of being unable to change what I had seen.

When I became pregnant myself, the nightmares returned with a force I wasn't prepared for. Night after night, I dreamt the same scene, seeing myself trying to reach out, trying to help. But no matter how hard I tried in those dreams, I could never get there in time. I'd wake up drenched in sweat, my hand often resting protectively on my belly, on my own child, overwhelmed by thoughts I couldn't control. Carrying my own children made me acutely aware of how deeply the fear of losing them had taken root within me.

Those dreams forced me to confront everything again, to face the guilt I carried for being able to escape, for continuing my life while others lost everything. But they also made me stronger. I realized that I couldn't bear the weight of the world's grief alone, that I had to find my own way to move forward.

I sit here, letting my thoughts drift between past and present, between the memories of what I witnessed and the reality I live now. The sorrow and guilt are still there, but they've found a new place within me. I've learned to live with them, and in some way, they've shaped me, becoming a part of the mother I am today – carrying my role with tenderness and care.

December 26, 2004
Matara, Sri Lanka

We ran until our legs felt like they would give out beneath us, adrenaline coursing through our veins, every breath burning in our chests. It felt as though we were fleeing from death itself. Each step took us farther from the danger, but we couldn't help glancing nervously over our shoulders, terrified of the next wave and how far it might reach.

Eventually, we came upon a large building—a towering, gray structure that loomed before us. It turned out to be a hospital under construction. Far from complete, but it offered refuge. It stood high above the ground, and to us, height meant safety.

We could hear shouts of "More waves! More waves!" as we rushed toward the entrance. Just as we were about to enter, a loud crash echoed behind us. Turning back, we saw two cars colliding in the chaos. One had lost control and hit a man standing at the side of the road. His body was thrown violently aside, like a rag doll tossed in the wind. I didn't see any more before we turned and hurried into the building, too scared of another wave, too frightened to linger and see what might happen next.

We took the stairs two at a time, our legs heavy and exhausted, but we kept climbing. Floor after floor, upward, always upward, as if we could escape the catastrophe by reaching higher ground. We were terrified, but also determined—we would survive this.

When we finally reached the roof, it felt like we'd stepped into another world. Under the gray sky, the roof was crowded with people. The injured and the shocked were scattered everywhere, their faces pale and empty, eyes filled with terror. Some were bloody, others seemed frozen in a state of disbelief, unable to comprehend what had just happened. A woman screamed in pain, fainting repeatedly, her cries cutting through the air like a knife, a stark reminder of the suffering surrounding us. A father, his eyes red and swollen, his face etched with despair, called out for his daughter, his voice cracked with desperation.

We found a corner where we could sit and try to collect our thoughts. Mom pulled out our water bottles, handing one each to me and Olof, and said we'd keep two for ourselves and share the others. We offered water to the dazed and traumatized people around us. Mom moved as if on autopilot, instinctively knowing that all we could do now was help each other, stay calm, and focus.

When the water ran out, she turned to a woman who seemed familiar with the building and asked cautiously if there was more water somewhere. The woman nodded gratefully, walking to the edge of the roof and pointing down toward a spigot on the street. The street seemed quiet now. The waves hadn't reached this far up, and cars were already heading back toward the beach, signaling that the latest wave had receded.

Mom decided to go down and refill the bottles, and I offered to help. Carefully and on edge, we made our way down the stairs and out onto the street. When we reached the spigot, protruding from the roadside, we began filling the bottles.

Everything was still, but it was a menacing stillness, as if we were all waiting for the next disaster. Just as we finished and turned to head back, a small girl approached Mom. She couldn't have been more than four years old, her wide, innocent eyes fixed on us. She said nothing, simply took Mom's hand and smiled—a silent, serene smile in the midst of all the chaos.

Mom tried speaking to her in English, asking where her parents were, but the girl didn't respond. She just stood there, quiet and motionless, as if she had found her own sense of safety in Mom's hand. We knew it wasn't safe to stay on the street, so we brought her back up to the roof with us. The situation there was just as chaotic as when we had left.

But then, something incredible happened. The man who had been calling for his daughter spotted the girl, and I watched as his face transformed from utter despair to relief and joy. His eyes widened, and without a word, he rushed toward her, scooping her into his arms and holding her so tightly it seemed he'd never let go. The girl smiled, finally understanding what was happening, and hugged him back. It was as if a spark of hope had ignited in the midst of all the darkness.

But the joy was short-lived.

Just seconds after the man let go of the girl, he began to scream uncontrollably again. His joy turned to despair in an instant, and he collapsed to the ground, pounding his fists against the rooftop. The girl recoiled, frightened, and cautiously returned to my mother, taking her hand again as if seeking the safety she had first found there.

The woman who had shown us where to find water explained with a sorrowful voice, "That's his daughter. But he just realized his wife is gone." Her words hit me like an icy wind. How could anyone cope with such a loss—to find your child again in one moment, only to realize that the other person you loved most in the world was lost forever? It was as if life gave and took in the same breath, a brutal reminder of how fragile everything was.

We sat there in silence, surrounded by people living through their own tragedies. No one dared to speak. I watched as my mother held the little girl's hand tightly, as if trying to shield her from the harsh reality we were all trapped in.

I'd lost count of time but not of the waves. I counted eight as we sat on the rooftop. Each time a wave receded, we could hear people below beginning to move again. They rushed toward the beach and the bus station, desperate to rescue loved ones or at least help those who were injured or trapped in the wreckage.

But every time, another wave came, bringing fresh panic. Cars that had driven toward the beach to help would make frantic U-turns, speeding away from the water. People who had started running down to the bus station would sprint back up toward higher ground. It was like a horrific game of hope and despair, with everyone trapped in a recurring nightmare. The sounds of sirens, screams, and cars reversing filled the air.

It's unclear how long we stayed up on that roof. Time felt unreal, as if the world had paused, and all we could do was wait. During that time, we handed out water to those around us, sharing what we had and trying to help however we could. The little girl, still holding my mother's hand, seemed to have found a sense of safety with us.

After a while, I took out the camera again. It felt strange to hold something so ordinary in such an extreme situation, but I showed the little girl how it worked. Her eyes lit up with curiosity, and she took a picture of me. I smiled at her, and she pointed to the camera and said something in Sinhala that I didn't understand. But her laughter was infectious.

Several people around us joined in her laughter, and a woman who spoke English smiled and said, "She thinks you're dirty." The woman pointed at my tank top, and I looked down. What had once been white was now covered in dirt and stains. I burst into laughter, and it felt as though something inside me broke free. It was so liberating to laugh, to feel something other than fear, even as everything around us was so uncertain. I hadn't even noticed how filthy I was, but now it was clear—my tank top looked as if I'd rolled in mud. I was dirty from head to toe.

My mother and Olof started laughing too, and I pointed at them. "You don't look any better!" I said, and we kept laughing together, as if trying to laugh away the fear for just a moment.

But my father didn't laugh. He stood off to the side, thoughtful, his eyes fixed on the horizon. His face was tense, and I knew he was thinking about what we should do next. He came over to us and said, "We need to move. We can't stay here any longer. We need food, water, and a safe place to sleep."

The rest of us nodded in agreement. There was no way to know how long we could stay on this roof, and with each passing hour, it became clear that we needed a more sustainable solution.

My father turned to my mother and said, "We'll split up. I'll take Olof and see if we can find somewhere to go. You two," he pointed at me, "stay here and keep an eye on our things."

I felt a knot tighten in my stomach. Splitting up felt dangerous, but we didn't have a choice. We had to be practical. My mother looked at me and gave a small, reassuring smile, but I could see that she was worried too.

"Be careful," she said to my father and Olof. "Come back as soon as you can."

My father nodded and gave us one last look before he and Olof disappeared down the stairs. My mother and I stayed behind, and an unsettling sense of vulnerability began to creep in. There was something about staying on the roof while they were gone that made everything feel even lonelier and more exposed.

My mother moved closer to me and put her arm around my shoulders. "We're going to get through this," she said softly. But I could see the worry in her eyes. Even though we didn't know exactly what had happened, we understood that the situation was dangerous. We knew that the people around us were desperate, and that access to food, water, and money could quickly become a matter of survival. All we could do now was wait and hope that my father and Olof would find a way forward.

Once again, I lost track of time. We had been sitting on the roof for what felt like an eternity, and now it was starting to get dark. The sky, still faintly lit by the setting sun, had shifted to a muted purple hue. Finally, after what seemed like hours, we saw my father and Olof coming back. They waved for us to come closer.

When they reached us, my father spoke in a low voice. "We've found a place to stay. We need to grab our things and leave now," he said. "We can't stay here any longer."

We tried to keep quiet as we gathered our belongings, but inside, it felt wrong. Leaving these people behind on the roof while we walked away felt like we were abandoning them. Like we were retreating back to a world where refrigerators were stocked with food and problems never felt this big.

As we packed up and prepared to leave, I noticed something out of the corner of my eye. The little girl's hand reached out for my mother. She hugged my mother tightly, then came over to me and hugged me too. Nothing was said. No words were exchanged—just silent goodbyes. We turned and began to make our way down the stairs, and I saw my mother wiping tears from her cheeks.

When we reached the street, my father led us away from the hospital building and the bus station. "We met a police officer," he said. "We're going to stay with him and his family. He's waiting for us down the road."

Two streets away, a man stood waiting. Even from a distance, we could see his cautious posture, his deeply lined face tense from the day's events. But as we approached, he greeted us with a kind smile despite his exhaustion.

We followed him through the quiet, empty streets, which now seemed almost deserted. It was as if the entire city was holding its breath after the day's chaos. We passed destroyed buildings and abandoned vehicles, but no one spoke. The silence was heavy, filled with thoughts none of us dared to put into words.

FIFTEEN

I quickly try to pull myself together, taking a deep breath and brushing the backs of my hands across my cheeks to erase the last traces of tears. I know my husband will soon notice my red, tear-streaked eyes, but I don't want to worry him. It feels silly, almost shameful, to sit here crying my heart out when so much in my life is good.

"Want some coffee?" he calls from the kitchen, where the sound of clinking dishes reveals his morning routine.

"Yes, please!" I reply, reaching for my empty cup to set it aside. His thoughtfulness warms me, and when he comes out with a steaming mug of coffee for me, I feel a pang of guilt for keeping my feelings to myself.

"Are you okay?" He looks at me with that expression, the one that can't be fooled by smiles or laughter. He knows me too well.

*I shake my head slightly, giving him a faint smile. "Yeah, it's just...
I spoke with Chamali yesterday, and it brought back so many
memories." I take a deep breath, trying to organize my thoughts.
"Sometimes it feels like I'm living two lives—this one, with you and
the kids, and another... far away, yet still so close. Everything that
happened, it shaped me, and yet I've never really talked about it."*

*He nods, sitting down beside me and taking my hand. "Of course.
Things like that don't just disappear." He runs his thumb gently
over the back of my hand, and I close my eyes, feeling the warmth of
his presence, the comfort.*

*I lean back, letting the warmth of the coffee seep into my cold hands.
"It feels strange," I say after a while. "Like I should be grateful for
surviving, for having the resources to come home, for being able to
move on as if nothing happened. But others... they were left to just
try and survive."*

*I fall silent, staring down into my coffee cup. He doesn't say
anything, but I know he's listening. And for the first time in a long
while, I feel that maybe—just maybe—I can start sharing
everything I've carried alone. Little pieces at a time, knowing that
he'll understand.*

December 26, 2004
Matara, Sri Lanka

After walking three more streets, the policeman, Ruwan, led
us into a small, lush garden that somehow seemed untouched
by the devastation just a few blocks away. The garden was
filled with the scent of wet earth, flowers, and rain, as if we
had stepped into another world—a place where time had

stopped, leaving chaos behind for a moment of peace. Ruwan opened a large, sturdy wooden door and gestured for us to enter his home. It was a simple but welcoming house, and the sense of safety was immediate as we crossed the threshold.

Inside, we were greeted by Ruwan's wife, Sumudu, a petite, warm woman with a broad smile that instantly made us feel at ease. Despite looking just as exhausted as we felt, there was a calming presence about her, something that soothed our tired, shaken spirits.

She spoke little English, but her laughter and eye contact conveyed a universal language that rendered words unnecessary. It was as if her demeanor reassured us that we were safe now.

They had two daughters, Chamali and Anjali, about the same age as Olof and me. The girls stood shyly in the doorway, offering hesitant smiles as we entered. It didn't take long for their shyness to give way to curiosity. With a child's eager fascination, they began to ask us countless questions about Sweden. They wanted to know about snow, how we celebrated Christmas, and what we ate at home. Their laughter filled the room, momentarily dispersing the heavy weight of disaster that hung over us all. To them, we seemed like exotic creatures, visitors from another world.

"You are welcome here," Ruwan said in a tired but genuine voice. "You are safe now." His words, simple but deeply meaningful, felt like a weight lifting off our shoulders. For the first time that day, I felt a genuine sense of relief. It wasn't over—we all knew that—but in that moment, we had found a place where we could breathe, if only for a while.

After we had sat down and caught our breath, Ruwan explained that he needed to return to the police station to assist but that we should stay here. Sumudu smiled and pointed toward the garden. "You can clean," she said, leading us to a makeshift outdoor shower made of a hose connected to a large water tank perched on a wooden stand. "Careful with the water," she added before leaving us there.

We understood that this was their only source of water and that we couldn't waste it. We tried to wash away the worst of the mud and grime from our bodies, using the water sparingly. Standing under the open sky, we dampened towels and scrubbed off as much as we could. I didn't get completely clean, but the feeling of fresh water on my skin was liberating.

After washing off some of the day's chaos, we felt slightly more human. The cold water revived us, and when we returned inside, we became acutely aware of our hunger. We hadn't eaten anything since breakfast that morning, and the growling in our stomachs was loud and insistent. Sumudu, with her constant smile and energetic demeanor, gestured toward the kitchen and invited us to help with dinner.

I was grateful for something practical to focus on after hours of panic and uncertainty. We helped peel vegetables and stir pots simmering on the gas stove. The scent of spicy curry and steaming rice filled the kitchen, and for a brief moment, it felt as if we were far removed from the catastrophe outside—just guests helping prepare a simple meal in someone's home.

The meal was humble, but at that moment, every smell and taste felt heightened, our hunger making us almost dizzy with anticipation. Olof and I exchanged glances across the kitchen, our stomachs growling loudly, barely able to wait for the food to be ready. When Ruwan returned from the police station just in time for dinner, a different kind of tension filled the room. He had news, but we tried to stay calm as we sat down at the table.

Just before we started eating, Ruwan sat heavily at the table and broke the silence with words that changed the entire atmosphere. "A tsunami has hit Sri Lanka," he said in a low, grave voice. His words hung in the air like a suffocating fog, and a sense of unreality washed over me. Tsunami. What did it even mean? I wasn't entirely sure, but I understood enough to know it was a violent force of nature, something beyond anything we could have imagined.

Ruwan continued, each word deepening the sense of chaos and devastation. "We were able to reach Colombo by satellite phone. It's not just here," he said, his gaze fixed on the table. "The destruction is widespread… Many villages have been washed away, and saltwater has infiltrated everything. Drinking water is now scarce, and the electricity won't return for a very long time."

I hadn't even realized there was no electricity until he said it, but now I noticed how dark everything was. Nothing illuminated our surroundings, except for the dim light of a single candle Sumudu had lit on the table.

Ruwan looked at us, his face hardened and lined by the shock of the day's events. The saltwater we had fled from hadn't just left death and destruction in its wake—it had also poisoned the very resources we all needed to survive. His voice grew darker as he explained the situation: "People are desperate. All the stores have already been looted. The shelves are empty, and the shops are destroyed. It's best we stay indoors."

His words hit like a series of blows to the chest. The image of people scrambling for the last bits of food, the last bottles of water, felt almost unreal. This was so far removed from our previous lives. But now, sitting there surrounded by chaos and despair, we slowly began to understand that this was our new reality.

A moment earlier, I had felt hunger, but now my appetite had vanished, as if something inside me had frozen solid. We sat still, silent, staring at our plates; no one moved their spoons. The food in front of us, which had earlier felt like a long-awaited comfort, suddenly seemed sacred.

I stared down at my plate, overcome by a sudden, heavy guilt. Guilt that we were sitting here with shelter and food while others were losing their homes—and maybe their lives—at that very moment. The thought of how fragile everything was, how quickly it could all be taken away, was overwhelming. What would happen tomorrow? Would anything be left at all?

No one dared to take the first bite. The food in front of us was undeniable proof of our vulnerability, a stark reminder that what we had always taken for granted—like food and water—was now fragile and far from guaranteed.

When Sumudu insisted that we begin eating, we did so hesitantly, as if every bite had to be measured. Every mouthful felt like a reminder of those who were perhaps fighting for their lives out there, searching for the food and water we now had before us.

I noticed how we all, without really discussing it, ate slowly, as if trying to stretch what was on our plates. There was something almost ritualistic about the meal, as though we knew it might be one of the last times we could eat without knowing when or if we'd have food again. Ruwan ate quietly, lost in thought, and Sumudu and the girls waited in the background. When we realized they wouldn't eat until we were finished, the meal became even heavier.

Every bite seemed to grow in my mouth, and I had to force myself to eat the little I had taken. Later, Chamali explained that this was a tradition in Sri Lanka. It was a way of showing respect through a specific hierarchy. Guests and the head of the family were served first, followed by the women and children. I felt uneasy seeing Sumudu, who had cooked the meal, standing there waiting for us to finish. Each bite felt like a reminder of the inequality between us, the guests, and them, the hosts who so generously shared the little they had.

It was as if the whole world had turned upside down in just a few hours, and now we had to navigate this new, fragile reality where every drop of water and every bite of food was precious. The question lingered in my mind: would we make it? Would we have anything to eat tomorrow, or would we, too, end up among those forced to loot to survive?

After the meal, Sumudu and the girls brought out their own plates and began eating quietly, almost ritualistically. They spoke softly to one another and occasionally glanced at us, as if to ensure we had had enough. Sumudu still smiled, but there was a deep exhaustion in her eyes that she couldn't hide. Ruwan said little during dinner, entirely absorbed in his thoughts, perhaps pondering what the next day would bring or what other disasters might yet unfold.

Despite the meal, which was genuinely delicious, dinner was somber. It was a quiet reminder that, although we were physically safe, we now lived in a world where every meal, every drop of water, was something we could no longer take for granted.

After dinner, we sat silently in the living room. We listened as Ruwan explained more about the situation. The phone lines were down, and those lucky enough to get a signal on their mobile phones were hearing horror stories from all directions. Entire families had lost everything. No one knew how many had died, and entire communities had been wiped away in moments.

"We're still trying to reach our families," Sumudu said, shaking her head faintly. She looked at her daughters, and I could feel the weight in her gaze. The desperate task of trying to contact loved ones, to find out who had survived and who hadn't, was a never-ending struggle. I could see how deeply tired she was, yet she kept her warm smile alive for us. It was as if she refused to let us see her break.

Even though Ruwan assured us that we were safe within these walls, we all felt the gravity of the situation. Every time a car passed on the street, every time the wind rustled through the garden, I wondered if we were truly safe. If another wave would come. If we would even have water to drink tomorrow. I could feel everyone's anxiety spreading like a silent, electric current through the room, but no one said a word. We just sat there, holding each other close, trying to make sense of what had happened and what was to come.

SIXTEEN

I realize how little I've actually processed the aftermath of the disaster. In the first few years, I mostly tried to suppress everything—bury the memories and shut off my emotions. Talking about it felt too hard, almost impossible. I never sought help, and no one really asked. It was as if everyone just expected me to move on, to handle it on my own. But deep down, I knew I never truly had.

I wonder if everything would have been different if I had received professional help. Maybe. Perhaps I could have gained a different perspective; perhaps someone could have helped me process the fear and guilt I've carried ever since. But there's no way of knowing. I moved forward in my own way, and for a long time, that meant running—running by pushing all my feelings aside.

The destructive behavior crept in gradually. At first, it was a relief to let go of everything for a while, to drink until the world felt distant and I became just a passenger in my own life. When I was drunk, I could, for a short moment, avoid thinking about what had happened, sinking into a haze where those memories couldn't intrude.

But soon it became a habit, something I longed for — to escape it all, even if just for an evening. I knew it wasn't sustainable, but at the time, I didn't care. Everyday life felt heavy and meaningless, and I found myself caught in a downward spiral where weekends often became an escape from my own memories.

It took time, and many missteps, before I slowly started to climb out of that destructive cycle. The memory of one particular night when I drank far too much and woke up the next morning with no memory of how I had gotten home became a turning point. It scared me and brought the realization that I couldn't keep living that way.

Over time, I came to understand that I could never drink myself free of the memories; they had only been pushed aside, not erased. I learned to carry them in other ways, to channel the pain into something else — my family, my work, my determination to build a life that truly meant something.

There, in the stillness of the morning, I felt a mix of sorrow and gratitude. Sorrow for having wasted so much time trying to run from my own pain, but gratitude for having found a way out, to a life that felt real and meaningful.

December 26, 2004
Matara, Sri Lanka

We were given Chamali and Anjali's room to stay in, and it felt like a privilege that they gave up their own beds for us. The room was simple yet vibrant, with small personal touches like stuffed animals and posters on the walls. The girls beamed as they helped us make the beds and showed us where we could put our belongings. Dusk was settling in, and with the electricity still out, it was growing harder to see.

But when it was time to go to bed, I was shocked. As I lay in the bed, looking up at the ceiling, I saw something that frightened me. The roof tiles, visible from inside because there was no insulation, had a pattern that resembled small swastikas. I sat up immediately.

"Olof, do you see that?" I whispered, pointing at the ceiling. "What kind of place is this?"

Olof stared up at ceiling, his face mirroring the alarm I felt. We lay there in the dark, silent and tense, the flickering shadows from outside dancing across the walls. My mind raced as I wondered what we had gotten ourselves into.

The door creaked open, and Dad stepped into the room, his expression calm but questioning. Without hesitation, I blurted out what we had seen, my voice trembling slightly as I tried to explain.

To our relief, Dad smiled. "That's nothing to worry about," he said calmly. "It's actually an ancient sun symbol, used long before the Nazis appropriated it and made it their own."

Dad explained that he had read about how many cultures around the world, including in Asia, had used a similar symbol for centuries as a representation of the sun god, good fortune, and prosperity. "It's just a coincidence that it looks like the Nazi swastika. Here, it has a completely different meaning."

I felt myself relax, and Olof sighed in relief. I had been on the verge of panicking over something I didn't understand, but now I felt almost embarrassed for being so scared.

With this new understanding from Dad, we stayed in bed, looking back up at the ceiling. The symbols on the tiles no longer seemed threatening. Instead, I began to see them as something ancient and significant, a part of a culture I didn't know but now had the chance to experience in a deeply personal way.

We lay close together in the upstairs room, trying to find some semblance of calm, but sleep remained elusive. Outside, the chaotic world grew even more frantic with the fall of night. The situation on the streets had taken a violent turn, and we could hear people shouting, their voices growing more desperate. Gunfire rang out suddenly, interrupting the sound of glass shattering as stores were looted for food and water. Several times, loud fights and frantic cries echoed through the streets, turning the area outside into what felt like a war zone.

Ruwan, who was sleeping with his family downstairs, had tried to reassure us earlier in the evening. "You're safe here," he had said, showing us his loaded service weapon and a rifle he kept by his bedside. His words, meant to comfort, instead filled us with unease. In his eyes, there was an unspoken fear, as if he knew that no weapon in the world could truly restore order. His family was as vulnerable as we were, and we all understood that danger was only a few meters beyond the front door.

Military helicopters roared above the city, their thunderous presence drowning out other sounds as they flew low over the rooftops. According to Ruwan, these were Indian military helicopters, ferrying injured people from a nearby soccer field to naval ships stationed along the coast in a desperate attempt to provide medical aid. I could imagine the helicopters lifting off into the darkness, their spinning blades a grim reminder that time was running out for many.

Inside the house, we lay there, listening to the terrifying chaos outside. Mom held me close, but her body was tense, and I could feel her fear as strongly as my own. Olof and Dad shared the other bed, and I heard Olof shifting restlessly, just as affected by the sounds and the atmosphere as I was. Every time a new burst of gunfire erupted or a helicopter passed overhead, we all froze. It was a constant reminder that the danger wasn't just out there—it was real, closer than we wanted to believe.

Throughout the night, the situation on the streets escalated. There was no place for us to feel safe or at ease, and even though we were surrounded by the kindness and protection of Ruwan's family, we were just as vulnerable as they were. The roar of helicopters, the desperate cries, and the sound of glass shattering filled our temporary sanctuary with the constant presence of looming danger. As dawn approached, none of us had slept much, but we clung to each other tightly—the only source of comfort in a night filled with fear.

The day after the tsunami, we were still deeply shaken, trying to comprehend what had happened. The chaos and riots of the night before had calmed, and we were attempting to adjust to life in Ruwan's home, where his family had welcomed us with such kindness and generosity. It felt as if we were in a bubble of calm, even though we knew the world outside had changed dramatically. Amid this restless state, Ruwan's eldest sister arrived for a visit, and her presence immediately shifted the atmosphere in the house.

Her arrival felt like a pivotal moment. It was clear she was the matriarch of the family, and her presence brought a sense of formality that hadn't been there before. She had a quiet authority that was immediately apparent. Everyone in the house, including Ruwan and Sumudu, directed their attention toward her and showed her deep respect. Despite the crisis outside the walls, she seemed to provide the family with a sense of stability and order.

She was older than Ruwan, and it was evident she had seen much in her life. Her face bore the marks of both experience and resilience, and though she didn't say much, it felt like every word she spoke carried weight. Sumudu and Ruwan listened intently when she spoke, while we, as guests, sat on the sidelines, trying to understand the dynamic unfolding before us.

The mood in the house was heavy. Every breath felt laden with the uncertainty and worry that still hung over us in the aftermath of the tsunami. Sumudu must have noticed our restlessness, as she leaned over and whispered something to her eldest daughter, Chamali. Chamali looked up, a mischievous smile spreading across her face, and waved us over.

"Come," she said brightly, as if she'd just come up with the best idea ever.

She disappeared into a small shed next to the house, rummaging through various items. After a few moments, she emerged holding four badminton rackets and a shuttlecock. "We'll play out here," she said, heading toward the street outside. Olof and I followed, hesitant at first, but drawn in by her enthusiasm.

The street outside was eerily empty. If it hadn't been for the shattered glass and what looked like bloodstains on one wall, it could almost have felt like a normal day. It was strange to think we were about to play badminton in a place still so visibly scarred by catastrophe. But Chamali seemed unfazed. She positioned herself on one side of the street, and when Anjali joined her, their energy was infectious.

The two girls turned out to be incredibly skilled at badminton. With effortless movements, they sent the shuttlecock flying back and forth between them as if it were the most natural thing in the world. Olof and I struggled to keep up—every time we tried to hit the shuttlecock, it either landed in the bushes or flew to the other side of the street. The girls laughed heartily at our clumsy attempts, but not in a mean way. Their laughter was contagious, and soon we were all laughing together.

It was surreal to play out there, with the shuttlecock soaring back and forth in an environment so heavily marked by destruction. The damage from the tsunami and the riots of the previous night were all around us—cracked walls, shattered windows, debris still scattered down the street. But in that moment, as we chased the shuttlecock and tried to keep it in the air, it felt as though time had stopped. The simplicity of the game gave us all a brief reprieve, a pause from everything that had happened and everything that lay ahead.

Chamali and Anjali moved with such confidence and skill that I almost felt envious. I glanced at Olof, who was struggling just as much as I was, and we exchanged a look of tired but happy resignation. They were far better than us, but it didn't matter. Their joy in playing was infectious, and for a little while, we were just kids having fun, not thinking about what had happened or what the next day would bring.

We played until it was nearly lunchtime. As we finally sat down to rest, sweaty and out of breath, I realized how much we'd needed to move, to let go of the tragedy and worry for a little while. Chamali and Anjali had given us more than just a moment of play—they had reminded us that even in a city struggling to rise again, life and joy could be found amidst the ruins.

As we caught our breath after the badminton match, the sound of approaching helicopters reached our ears again. We looked up to see one flying low overhead, following its path as it roared across the sky.

Suddenly, we saw Ruwan rushing out of the house with Mom and Dad close behind. He waved at us urgently.

"It's the vice president!" Ruwan shouted. "Hurry!"

Confused and filled with adrenaline, we scrambled to our feet and ran after him. We followed the helicopter as it disappeared further away, heading toward the same soccer field the Indian army had used the night before to transport the injured. Breathless and with our hearts pounding, we reached the field just in time to see not one, but four helicopters landing. Their rotor blades were deafening, drowning out any attempt at conversation.

As the helicopters touched down, soldiers began pouring out—at least ten from each chopper, all armed and on high alert. It was an overwhelming sight, and we stood frozen, wide-eyed, watching the scene unfold. From the fourth helicopter, the one bearing a large golden lion emblem, a well-dressed man stepped out, speaking on his mobile phone. It was clear he was someone important, as the soldiers formed a protective perimeter around him.

Before we could process what was happening, Dad suddenly sprinted toward the man. "I need to borrow your phone! I need to borrow your phone! I can pay you!" he shouted, his voice rising above the noise of the helicopters. The soldiers reacted instantly, raising their weapons toward him.

In that moment, panic surged through us. Ruwan and his daughters threw themselves to the ground, arms over their heads, while we stood frozen in terror. The situation turned deadly serious in the blink of an eye. My heart raced as I stood there, paralyzed with fear.

Had we survived a tsunami only to watch our father get shot on a soccer field? Would we all be gunned down by the military? I didn't dare breathe.

Perhaps it was our pale skin and the fact that we were tourists that saved us from an even worse situation. The man, who turned out to be Sri Lanka's vice president, eventually seemed to grasp our desperation and raised his hand to calm his soldiers. Slowly, they lowered their weapons, though their icy gazes remained unyielding.

Dad pleaded again, his voice filled with urgency, asking to borrow the phone. The well-dressed man looked at us with a mixture of curiosity and understanding. He seemed to realize that Dad wasn't a threat but rather a panicked father desperate to secure his family's safety.

Despite the absurdity of the situation, we were finally allowed to borrow the phone from the man, who indeed introduced himself as the vice president of Sri Lanka. We barely reacted to this revelation, our full attention focused on the phone. I remember Dad's hands trembling as he dialed the number for Sweden. We all huddled together, waiting for the call to connect, and it felt as if time itself had stopped.

When the call finally went through, and after what felt like an eternity, we heard Grandma's voice on the other end. It was as if the weight of the past few days lifted all at once. Tears streamed down Mom's face as we told Grandma we were safe. Hearing her voice and sensing her relief was one of the most comforting moments I had ever experienced. Grandma assured us that she would inform the rest of the family back home that we were okay. The call was brief, but it was enough to give us the strength we needed to keep moving forward.

After the call with Grandma, Dad contacted the Swedish embassy. They advised us to make our way there as soon as possible and promised to do everything they could to assist us further. However, their response lacked a full understanding of the severity of the situation, but we resolved to follow their advice and head there as soon as we could.

The vice president, visibly relieved that the situation hadn't escalated, approached us again. He offered a kind smile and suggested that we could stay in his summer home in the mountains until things calmed down. It was an incredibly generous offer—a safe place far from the chaos of the coast. He described the house as large and comfortable, with enough food and water to sustain us for as long as needed. "But you need to find a car and drive there by yourself, since I need to continue working, as you understand," he said, gesturing broadly toward the soccer field.

I followed his gesture with my eyes and only then realized what was stacked around the edges of the field.

I staggered. They were bodies.

Ruwan explained later that evening that the vice president's visit to the town was primarily to decide how to deal with the thousands of bodies now filling the city.

Despite the goodwill behind the vice president's offer to lend us his summer home, it felt wrong. We just wanted to go home. We didn't want to stay any longer than absolutely necessary, no matter how comfortable it might have been. The tsunami had torn us apart internally in ways we didn't yet fully understand, and while we knew we couldn't immediately return to Sweden, we wanted to get to the embassy as soon as possible. We needed to feel like we were heading home, back to something familiar and safe, even though the world itself had irrevocably changed.

"Thank you, but we just want to go home," Dad said politely but firmly, and I could see the relief in his face when the vice president nodded in understanding.

After saying goodbye to the vice president and his escort, we began the slow walk back to Ruwan's house. The soldiers remained by the helicopters, and the sound of the rotor blades filled the air again as we walked away. It was as if everything that had just happened was part of an unreal dream, but the comfort of having spoken to Grandma and receiving instructions from the embassy made it easier to breathe.

On the way back, it felt as though we had taken a step closer to leaving all this devastation behind. Thoughts of going home made us feel lighter, even though we knew the journey was far from over.

SEVENTEEN

I sat there in the car, staring out through the windshield while my thoughts swirled. I tried to focus on the road, but the memory of my daughter's tiny hands clinging to my neck wouldn't leave me. I had rushed through the drop-off at preschool, quickly passing her over to one of the teachers and waving briefly while trying to ignore the tears in her eyes. Now, I felt a lump in my own throat, and the sting of tears burned behind my eyelids. Everything I had—two healthy children, an amazing husband, a safe home, running water, electricity, access to food—such simple things that I so often forgot to appreciate.

My thoughts drifted back to the time when we lived in the tiny guesthouse, without running water, while we were building the house. I was pregnant with our youngest then, and every day felt like a battle to make things work. It had been hard, but we had always had options. We could shower at the gym, and there was water in the tap, even if it was a little ways away. But sitting there in the car, I realized just how small those challenges had been compared to the conditions I had witnessed after the tsunami in Sri Lanka.

The memories were as vivid now as they had been then. The image of the crowd at the gas station returned to me. How Ruwan, our friend and savior, had had to show his police badge just so we could get a chance to refuel. People had stood in line for hours, maybe days, hoping for just a few liters of gasoline. I remembered how desperate everyone was, how their faces carried that same expression of worry and hope, yearning to get somewhere else—away from the devastation, away from hunger, away from the scarcity of clean water.

What we considered basic essentials—water, gasoline, food—were life-or-death resources there. In Sri Lanka, after the tsunami, the water was poisoned by salt, and everywhere around us, stores and homes were being looted—not out of malice, but sheer desperation. Sitting here now, in a comfortable car on my way to a job I had worked so hard to get, I felt so far removed from all of it.

I sighed, feeling the guilt gnawing at me. How could I have all this now, when the people I met in Sri Lanka might still be struggling with loss and hardship? What does my job even mean, really? Is it worth rushing off every morning, leaving my crying daughter behind?

December 27, 2004
Matara, Sri Lanka

Getting to the Swedish Embassy in Colombo turned out to be easier said than done. Although we now had a plan and a destination, it became clear that the journey there would be both long and uncertain. Ruwan, who had been out speaking with local authorities and others in the town, returned with news that made us grasp the true gravity of the situation.

"All the roads along the coast are washed away," he explained with a heavy sigh. "And not just the roads—the railway tracks have been swept away by the water too. The entire infrastructure has collapsed." His worried expression as he continued speaking quickly made us realize that our journey to the embassy would not be simple.

The coastal route, normally one of the fastest ways to Colombo, was no longer passable. Every road leading to the capital had been obliterated by the massive tsunami waves that had rolled in, destroying everything in their path. The mental images that began forming in our minds—of stranded cars, overturned trains, and collapsed bridges—made the trip feel more and more hopeless.

"But what about the mountains?" my father asked, his tone tinged with hope. "Is there any road through the mountains that's still passable?"

Ruwan shook his head. "It's hard to say. Before the tsunami, we had heavy rains in the mountains. The downpour was so severe that the roads there were undermined, and in several places, parts of the roads have been washed away too. It's possible that some routes are still impassable, but we've heard that there's one path that might still work."

Despite the dire situation, there was a glimmer of hope. Sumudu's brother, who lived in Colombo, was making his way to Matara via the mountains. He had been on the road for hours, and if he managed to make it all the way, it would mean there was a viable route back to Colombo.

"If he makes it, we'll know that you can take that route," Ruwan said, trying to reassure us. "It would mean you could avoid the coast entirely and drive through the mountains instead."

But we could all feel the uncertainty hanging in the air. We waited for news about Sumudu's brother, not knowing if we could even move forward. The storm damage in the mountains and the destroyed roads made every step of the journey feel precarious. The situation was unpredictable, and while we had a plan, it was a fragile one.

It felt strange to sit there, sheltered in Ruwan and Sumudu's home, trying to figure out how we could reach the safety of Colombo when everything around us seemed so unstable. All we could do was hope for good news that Sumudu's brother had made it through the mountains and that the road was still passable.

Until then, we were stuck in uncertainty. It felt like we were in a vacuum—the desire to go home and start recovering from what we had experienced was strong, but the road there was littered with obstacles. The tsunami hadn't just destroyed buildings and roads; it had shaken our confidence in how the world worked. We no longer knew what to expect.

Meanwhile, amid this uncertainty, Sumudu's brother became our last link to a possible way forward. If he made it, so could we. And if there was a road through the mountains, it might give us the freedom we needed to leave this place and begin our journey home.

That same afternoon, Olof and I accompanied Chamali and Anjali as they walked around the town to pay their respects to relatives and friends who had perished in the tsunami. It was a day filled with both sorrow and quiet reflection, where every step felt like part of a slow process of mourning. We walked along narrow streets between houses, through neighborhoods still bearing so many scars from the disaster. All around us were signs of destruction—homes that had been washed away, damaged roads, and people sitting outside their homes, their expressions empty and exhausted.

Chamali and Anjali led us silently, and we followed them as strangers in a world we couldn't fully comprehend. When we arrived at the homes of those who had passed away, we witnessed a part of Sri Lankan culture that was both beautiful and deeply moving. In Sri Lanka, it is customary for the deceased to be placed in their homes after death, often on the kitchen table. The body is surrounded by flowers, as if encased in the most beautiful gifts nature has to offer. It was a sight that felt both calming and overwhelming.

In the Western world, death is often kept at a distance, something that happens in hospitals or churches. But here, in the heart of the village, death was a present reality. It became part of the home, where the remaining family members and friends could grieve in an intimate and personal way. The flowers surrounding the body filled the room with a soft, sweet fragrance, creating a stark contrast to the heavy sorrow that lingered in the air. There was no distance between life and death—they existed side by side.

Following Chamali and Anjali as they went from house to house to bid farewell to their relatives and friends was an eye-opening experience for us. At each house, we stopped and stood silently and respectfully as the young girls bowed their heads in gestures of grief and reverence. We soon realized that this wasn't just a tradition—it was a way of preserving the memory of the deceased, ensuring they remained a part of the family even after their lives had ended.

We came to understand that funeral rituals in Sri Lanka are deeply embedded in the culture, varying slightly depending on religion and tradition, but always grounded in respect for the dead and a focus on community. We knew that the majority of Sri Lanka's population is Buddhist, and in Buddhism, funeral rituals hold a significant role. When someone passes away, it is essential to generate good karma by honoring them with a dignified funeral. The body is carefully washed and placed in the home, where family and friends can pay their final respects. Often, the body is surrounded by flowers and candles, symbolizing the impermanence of life and the rebirth that Buddhism teaches.

It was both beautiful and unsettling to witness these rituals up close. For Olof and me, who had barely attended funerals before, it was overwhelming to experience them so intimately. There was something deeply human about the way they handled grief—allowing the deceased to remain surrounded by their loved ones as if they were still a part of the home. It felt like a tribute to life and, at the same time, a reminder of its fragility.

We visited house after house, meeting families in mourning. They had lost so much, yet it seemed they understood that this was part of life's cycle. Children often sat near the deceased bodies, not afraid but seemingly accustomed to the idea that death is a natural part of existence. It was touching to see how they dealt with loss—not by pushing it away but by integrating it into their lives.

When we returned to Ruwan and Sumudu's home after our walk through the village, we were quiet. What we had seen and experienced weighed heavily on us, but at the same time, it felt as though we had gained a deeper understanding of how other cultures approach death. It was a reminder that life, no matter how fragile, always finds a way to continue. Here, the deceased were not left alone—they remained present in their homes, surrounded by flowers and love.

Dinner that evening reflected a subtle shift in hierarchy. Ruwan's sister, now present, took her place as the family matriarch, and she was led to the table first. Having traveled some distance, she decided to stay the night. The evening meal was special—Sumudu laid out the usual small dishes, but she also prepared a signature curry fish dish that was Ruwan's sister's favorite. We were offered a taste and, out of politeness, each took a small bite. That was all it took—just one bite to make our eyes water and our mouths burn from the heat.

We struggled to keep our composure, but Sumudu and the girls couldn't hold back their laughter as they watched us valiantly attempt to eat without betraying how overwhelmed we were by the spice. Their joyous laughter filled the room as we nodded appreciatively and quickly swallowed to ease the fiery sensation. One bite of the fish was enough for us—any more would have been unbearable.

The dish clearly held a special place in the family, and although I could hardly handle the spice, I did my best to show respect. The experience became a moment of connection and laughter, with Sumudu appearing as entertained as we were by our efforts to endure the spiciest food we had ever encountered.

Late that evening, Sumudu's brother, Nimal, arrived on his motorbike, bringing with him the same warm and infectious energy as his sister. Despite the chaos enveloping the country, he seemed tirelessly optimistic. He parked the heavily loaded motorbike in the yard and entered the house, full of energy, even though he had been traveling for hours on treacherous roads. We hurried outside to unload supplies from his bike, ensuring they were safely stored to avoid the risk of looting.

"The roads are tough," Nimal said in halting English, flashing his signature smile, "but we'll make it." His optimism gave us a sliver of hope amidst the darkness. He promised to drive us the next day, provided we could secure enough fuel. It sounded simple when he said it, but we knew the logistics in this situation were anything but straightforward.

Nimal had a friend in Matara who owned a minivan. This friend, also seeking to get to Colombo, agreed to take us along. Despite the growing hope of finally starting our journey home, the night brought little relief. As darkness fell, the unrest outside intensified, turning into outright chaos. I was terrified. We had food, water, and money inside the house. Did the armed mobs outside know that? Helicopters continued their relentless flights, and gunfire echoed more frequently, the intervals between salvos shrinking.

When dawn broke, it felt liberating. It was as though the city itself took a breath of calm before the rooster crowed—or perhaps I had managed to fall asleep briefly without realizing it. Either way, the new day had arrived, and at last, we were preparing to leave.

Early that morning, the minivan pulled up in front of the house. Only then did we realize it wasn't a typical passenger vehicle—it had been modified for transporting goods and resembled a cargo van more than anything else. There were only two actual seats, while the rest of the interior had been converted for carrying materials and supplies.

"We'll make it work," Nimal said with his usual smile. He and his friend quickly set up two planks in the cargo area, which we would use as makeshift benches. It was far from comfortable, but in our situation, it felt like a luxury simply to have a way out. The planks at least gave us somewhere to sit, and we were willing to endure any discomfort for the chance to leave Matara.

Fueling the vehicle proved to be an even greater challenge than we had anticipated. As we walked toward the gas station with two jerry cans to fill, the depth of the crisis became evident. The line stretched for hundreds of meters along the road, filled with restless people clutching their fuel cans tightly, hoping for their turn. Ruwan motioned for us to stay close to him. I noticed he had strapped on his service pistol and had his police badge ready as he strode purposefully past the long line of desperate people. We did our best to keep pace, passing the increasingly frustrated crowd, whose anger grew when they saw us skipping the queue.

As we approached the gas station itself, I saw that it was cordoned off by the military and police. Ruwan presented his credentials to the officer in charge, and we were allowed through the barricade.

I didn't fully understand what was happening. These people had been waiting for hours, perhaps even days, for enough fuel to escape this place that felt increasingly forgotten by the outside world, yet no one was allowed access. Further down the line, a violent fight broke out; we saw a young man brutally beaten after attempting to steal some fuel. The panic was palpable, like a heavy blanket smothering everyone waiting in line. Without fuel, they were trapped here, and with no food or water, it was only a matter of time before the situation grew even more dire.

The sight of an excavator rumbling to life next to me startled me, snapping me out of my thoughts. I hadn't noticed the massive machine being refueled, but now it was ready to move.

"Dad," I whispered, "what's going on?"

"They've shut down all the gas stations," he explained. "Only the police and military are allowed to collect fuel."

It felt profoundly unfair. Many of the people here had been waiting countless hours, and we could feel their resentful and envious stares boring into us. Yet we also knew that this might be our only chance—not just for us but for Ruwan's family as well. If we could leave, it would ease the burden on them. We understood that Sumudu and Ruwan had already shared everything they had with us, and every extra day we stayed meant more resources stretched thin.

With the van now refueled, we were ready to leave Matara. It felt like a weight had been lifted, but the guilt lingered. We knew we had been given an advantage that many others in the queue didn't have. Yet, in that moment, survival took precedence—and we had to seize the opportunities given to us.

EIGHTEEN

In the middle of one of today's meetings, where the conversation revolved around numbers and strategies, I realized I had had enough. The values in the room stood in stark contrast to what I personally believed to be important—the things that truly matter in life. Suddenly, the room felt stifling, the air heavy, and I stopped hearing the words being said. Compared to the insights I had carried with me from past trials, everything around me now seemed shallow and meaningless.

My thoughts drifted back to the night before, when memories of Sri Lanka had washed over me. There, amidst the chaos following the tsunami, I had seen both the worst and the best in humanity—a reality where there was no room for superficial conflicts or power struggles. Life was about survival, about holding on and supporting one another.

The meeting continued, but I slowly stood up, gathered my things, and approached the CEO. "I need to talk to you," I said in a calm but resolute voice. We left the room, and once we were in the quiet hallway, I said what I had been holding in for weeks, maybe even months.

"I'm resigning," I said without hesitation.

The shock on his face almost made me smile, but I maintained my firm tone. "I can't be part of this anymore—this is so far from what's important to me. I've realized I want to spend my time and energy on something that truly matters."

As I left the office, I felt a sense of relief I hadn't experienced in a long time. The air outside felt almost surreal, and as I walked toward my car, a growing sense of freedom built within me, stronger with each step.

On the drive home, as the scenery blurred past, I picked up my phone and dialed my husband's number.

"Hi, love," I said, unable to hide the light and excited tone in my voice.

"Hey! How's it going?" he asked cheerfully.

"You know, I resigned."

There was silence on the line for a second, but I could almost hear his smile spreading. "You did? It's about time!"

I laughed softly. "Yes. Finally. It was time. I can't be part of all that anymore. The bickering and the petty arguments—I have no energy left for it. I want to spend my time and energy doing something that actually matters."

We talked for a while about my decision, about how long I had been holding it in, and when we hung up, I felt stronger. I didn't know exactly what lay ahead, but one thing was certain—I was free from what had been weighing me down, and I was ready to create something of my own. Something that truly mattered.

December 28, 2004
Matara, Sri Lanka

And so, the time came to say goodbye. I had lost track of how long we had stayed with Ruwan, Sumudu, and their daughters. I think it was only two nights, but in the chaotic world we were living in, it felt like an eternity. Despite the short time, we had become part of their lives, and they part of ours, in a way that only happens in extreme circumstances. We had shared meals, laughter, and moments of despair, and there was a sense of mutual respect and gratitude lingering in the air as we prepared to leave.

When it came time to part ways, words felt inadequate. We hugged, bowed, and nodded to show our appreciation and respect in every way we could think of. Ruwan and Sumudu had opened their home to us at our most vulnerable, and now we were leaving them in the midst of their own struggle to return to something resembling normal life. They had shared everything they had with us, and no gesture seemed enough to express our gratitude.

We left most of the money we had with them—everything that hadn't already gone toward buying fuel and paying for our spot in the minivan. We knew they needed the money more than we did. It was a small gesture, but it was the only way we could show our appreciation for their generosity and warmth. The money wouldn't change their lives, but we hoped it would help them in the immediate future, as food and water supplies began to run out in the city.

As we sat in the rattling minivan and began to drive out of Matara, the extent of the tsunami's destruction became even more apparent. The roads were lined with mass graves—hastily dug and filled with bodies, as if the scope of the catastrophe had been too overwhelming for people to even have time to mourn. I looked at these trenches in the ground and was reminded of history lessons about World War II, the mass graves dug to manage the overwhelming death tolls in camps and on battlefields. This was different, yet what I saw now bore an eerie resemblance to those historical images—piles of bodies lying in rows beside large holes in the earth. This was a forced farewell, with no time for respect or rituals.

The bodies were shrouded in simple cloths, while others lay exposed, wrapped only in the clothes they had been wearing when the wave struck. Workers and military personnel moved briskly between the rows of graves and the massive excavators, their urgency palpable. It was as if every second mattered. Now I understood why only excavators had been permitted through at the gas station—time was critical. The bodies had to be buried before decomposition began, and the relentless heat made the task even more pressing.

I looked at the workers' faces, etched with exhaustion and strain. Their eyes were hollow, their movements mechanical, as though they had stripped away every emotion, driven solely by the raw instinct to keep going.

I thought of what Ruwan had said about stagnant water being contaminated with salt, and how bacteria could spread rapidly in this tropical heat. I understood that this was an attempt to protect the health of the survivors. There was no choice but to bury the bodies quickly and efficiently.

But there was something deeply unjust about the sight. These people would never receive proper burials. Families would never know exactly where their loved ones lay, and most would not even get the chance to say goodbye. The memory of these mass graves would linger as a collective grief for generations—a place where names, stories, and memories were buried in the earth without the chance for individual acknowledgment.

The heavy smell of ruined lives mixed with the dust and the smoke from Nimal's cigarette. We sat silently in the minivan, none of us saying a word. What could be said? It felt as if any words would be too small to capture what we were seeing and feeling. The tsunami had taken so many lives, and we were among the lucky ones who had survived. The sense of survival was mixed with deep sorrow for the lives lost.

As we passed some of the improvised grave sites, we saw people standing and looking down at the ground, their faces filled with grief and resignation. It was as if the world had stopped, and we were moving through a frozen image of devastation and human tragedy. People climbed among swollen and battered bodies, hoping to find their loved ones—or perhaps hoping not to find them. Children sat beside their deceased parents, while elderly men and women stood with empty gazes at the edges of the makeshift mass graves. It was a scene of chaos and loss, one I would never be able to forget.

Now, more than ever, I understood how lucky we had been. We had survived and been helped by people who were themselves fighting to survive. But survival came at a price—carrying these images and memories, feeling the guilt that comes with having made it through when so many others had not. It was too much to take in. I closed my eyes in a hopeless attempt to erase the sights from my mind.

The minivan rattled on, and as we left Matara behind, I knew we weren't just leaving a city in ruins—we were leaving behind a part of ourselves. We were leaving friends we might never see again, and we were leaving a place that had changed us forever.

NINETEEN

The cold autumn air seeps through my jacket, jolting me out of my thoughts. Once again, I've been lost in reflections on the past, on the immense guilt that has followed me through the years. A guilt that, like a faint but persistent echo, has pulsed within me ever since I returned from Sri Lanka. Why me? Why was my family allowed to return to safety, while so many others were left behind?

I remember the surreal feeling of leaving the chaos behind. Boarding a plane and returning to Sweden, coming home to a life where water, electricity, and food were never in question. An unimaginable luxury, I realize now, but one I took for granted back then. How many times have I thought of those who never had that opportunity? Of all the people left behind, trapped in a world full of loss, devastated by a force of nature no one could stop.

The inner voice constantly whispers about the guilt I feel toward those who died, those who lost their loved ones—both the ones who were there and those sitting at home in Sweden who lost someone they cared about. So many lives were lost in the pursuit of a few weeks of paradise, while I merely had to pack my backpack and fly home.

When I reflect deeper, I realize another side of this guilt. There's a sadness that has lived in me for so long, but sometimes it feels like I have no right to grieve. After all, my family survived. We're all alive, and after the disaster, we returned to a safety many will never experience. What do I really have to be sad about? Why should I feel such deep sorrow when my story, in the end, had a happy ending?

Yet it lingers, and I understand now that it's this unresolved feeling of guilt and sorrow that has held me back for so long. But why must I feel guilty just because I feel sad when the memories resurface? Is it really wrong to feel sorrow, even when I was lucky enough to survive? I'm beginning to understand that my grief is just as real as anyone else's, even if it looks different.

Perhaps it's time to let go of the guilt. I will always carry the memories of Sri Lanka, but maybe I can start to accept them. After all, I know it wasn't my fault. The natural disaster, the wave, the deaths—none of it was within my control. I was given a second chance, and the only thing I can do is live with that knowledge.

December 28, 2004
Matara, Sri Lanka

Hour after hour, we traveled along rough roads, surrounded by a landscape that was both wild and breathtaking. The roads were bumpy and riddled with potholes, and with every jolt, it felt like I sank deeper into the hard wooden plank we were sitting on. That day, I gained a new appreciation for the phrase "pain in the rear," as the ache in my back and legs grew with every kilometer.

Occasionally, we passed military vehicles marked with red crosses, transporting the injured and vital supplies. Their presence was a sobering reminder of the gravity of the situation, yet it all felt strangely distant as we moved through the incredibly beautiful surroundings. Outside the vehicle, tea plantations stretched out alongside dense jungle as far as the eye could see. Everything was so lush and vibrant, as if the nature here existed in stark defiance of the devastation we had left behind.

I tried to focus on the stunning scenery rather than the discomfort in my body. I saw farmers working in the fields, carrying on despite the drastic changes in the world around them. The jungle felt endless, with its dense trees and plants reaching skyward. Every part of the landscape seemed to have its own rhythm, one that stood in sharp contrast to the chaos and destruction we had escaped in Matara.

At one point, we all had to get out of the van. A section of the road had been washed away by earlier monsoon rains, and the vehicle couldn't cross on its own. Without hesitation, we all pitched in to push the van over the damaged section of road. It was physically demanding but a welcome break from sitting, and the teamwork gave us a brief sense of solidarity—we were all determined to keep moving forward, no matter what it took.

I don't know how long we traveled through the mountains, but by the time we reached Colombo, it was late. We were exhausted, hungry, and filthy, with every part of our bodies aching from the long journey.

As we entered the city, we were met with a sight that was haunting. White strips of cloth hung everywhere—along streets, from trees, and on lampposts. They fluttered gently in the evening breeze, creating an eerie, somber atmosphere.

Nimal, seated next to the driver, turned around and noticed my puzzled expression. "It's an old tradition," he explained calmly. "White cloth is hung to honor the dead. It's our way of showing respect and mourning those we've lost."

I nodded silently, but the sight of so many white strips knotted something deep within me. It wasn't just a few ribbons—they were everywhere, hundreds, maybe thousands of them. Each one represented a life taken, a family now in mourning. I couldn't stop staring at them. The way the ribbons swayed in the breeze seemed to tell stories—of sudden deaths, chaos, and how quickly life could change. A constant reminder of the sorrow and loss that permeated the entire country. It was as if the city itself was grieving, with every street and building carrying a silent burden of suffering.

It felt surreal to see this large city, bustling with people, continuing its daily routines amidst such devastation. Life went on, but grief was palpable—not just in the white ribbons but in people's faces, their slow steps, and quiet conversations.

Nimal remained silent, but I noticed how he occasionally glanced out the window, as though each ribbon reminded him of something he would rather forget.

When the minivan finally pulled up in front of the Swedish embassy, we embraced Nimal goodbye. He had been our savior, a vital link in the lifeline that had brought us through the country. We thanked him and the driver profusely before they disappeared into the growing darkness.

Outside the embassy stood a guard in a small booth. After showing our passports, we were let in. It felt strange to stand there in front of the high, solid gates, about to step into a world far removed from the destruction and grime we had just left behind. As we walked through the gates, I felt out of place. The hedges were trimmed into perfect squares, and the lawn was improbably pristine, especially given the chaos we had experienced in Matara. The contrast was staggering. We followed the path to the grand building, our steps heavy with fatigue, and finally stepped inside.

The embassy's interior was sterile and sparse. In the waiting room, separated by a large glass wall, a woman sat eating a banana, seemingly oblivious to our arrival. Exhausted and starving, we watched her and hoped she might offer us something. But the offer never came, and none of us had the courage to ask.

In the waiting room, a young couple sat looking as worn and defeated as we felt. They had lost everything—everything except the tattered clothes on their backs. We overheard the woman behind the glass instructing them to fill out forms to borrow money from the embassy and apply for new passports. That was their only way to get home. I stared at them, wondering what kind of place this was. Wasn't an embassy supposed to be a sanctuary, a place to turn to when you were most in need?

When it was our turn, we explained that, following the embassy's recommendation, we had made our way all the way there. Fortunately, we still had our passports and some money—something we now understood was more than many others had. The woman behind the glass looked at us and replied dryly, "Well, then there's not much more we can do for you." She paused briefly before continuing, "We can recommend a nice hotel and a nearby restaurant if you're hungry."

Dad, already exhausted and frustrated, looked at her with a mixture of confusion and irritation. "Can't we sleep here?" he asked.

"No, of course not," she replied without even blinking. "But this hotel is good, and they have an excellent restaurant too." She handed over a brochure, as if it was the most obvious solution in the world.

"Are there any flights home?" Dad finally blurted out, his voice sharper now as he regained the ability to speak, clearly more irritated.

"We don't know," the woman responded with the same indifference. "But you can go to the airport for further instructions."

When we stepped back out onto the street, Dad was furious. "I have never seen such terrible service!" he exclaimed. We all agreed, but our exhaustion made it hard to articulate just how disappointed we felt. We began walking toward the restaurant and hotel that had been recommended to us. When we arrived and stood in front of the enormous, luxurious building, it felt like we had entered a completely different world. The staff, dressed in suits, gave us peculiar looks, their eyes lingering on our dirty clothes and worn faces. I was so tired and drained that I barely recognized my reflection in the large glass windows, and I felt utterly out of place in these extravagant surroundings.

"We can't go in there," Mom said firmly. "It feels wrong when so many people don't even have food on the table." We all nodded in agreement. Sitting down at a fancy restaurant while people just miles away were fighting for their survival felt completely absurd.

"Let's try heading to the airport instead," Dad said, attempting to flag down a taxi. Maybe the airport could provide the help we needed—not just to get home but to make sense of everything we had just experienced.

TWENTY

That evening, as calm settled over the house and the children lay sleeping, I felt a knot of anxiety growing in my stomach. The panic had started creeping in on the way home, but I had pushed it aside, trying to stay calm. Now, in the stillness, it hit me with full force. What had I done? Resigning, just like that. It had felt right in the moment, but now it seemed almost unrealistic, like an impulsive decision I might come to regret. Damn it, why did I always have to be so impulsive? I cursed myself.

I sat at the kitchen table with my hands clasped in front of me, staring at them as if they held the answers I needed. Without my high salary—what would happen then? I pictured the bills, the children's activities, our family's everyday life. Would we have to give all that up? It felt heavy, almost like a wall had risen in front of me, blocking all paths forward, and the whole situation felt utterly hopeless.

Just then, my husband came into the room. He immediately noticed something was wrong, sat down beside me, and placed his hand over mine. "Of course, we'll manage," he said softly. I thought for a moment. "What do you think about renting out the house for a while and moving back into the guest house?" We had done it once before—lived in the guest house while the house was being built. Sure, living in such a small space was challenging, but we had managed it. And it has brought us closer, giving us moments of real connection.

"Let's do it," he replied. "We'll see it as an adventure."

I felt so grateful to him and a little lighter in spirit. But the doubts still churned in the back of my mind, and I knew they wouldn't disappear overnight.

December 28, 2004
Matara, Sri Lanka

In the taxi on the way to the airport, Dad was furious. "How the hell can they recommend a damn luxury hotel when the country is in ruins?" Mom sat silently, nodding in agreement, her eyes filled with tears. She hadn't said much in the past few days. Neither had Olof.

It was past midnight now, and as we approached the terminal, it became clear that we were not the only ones trying to leave Sri Lanka. The area was bustling with activity, as though the whole world had converged in one place. Yet, despite the crowd, the atmosphere was subdued. A heavy, almost oppressive calm hung in the air, and few people spoke above a whisper.

162

At the airport entrance, flight attendants in smart uniforms handed out water bottles and plastic-wrapped sandwiches to each arriving passenger. They stood there with dazzling smiles, though their tired eyes betrayed the long hours they must have worked. They also provided clear instructions to everyone arriving. "All passengers with passports, please line up to the right," they said kindly but firmly. "All passengers without passports, please line up to the left." Their efficiency was impressive, almost military-like in its precision. No one questioned or protested—everyone simply followed instructions.

Despite the flurry of activity, the airport was eerily quiet. People whispered to one another, and many stood silently, exhausted and physically drained from the past days' events. We followed the instructions and joined the line for passport holders. It felt as though we were all part of something larger, an unspoken understanding that we had survived and now just wanted to go home.

Standing in line, I suddenly spotted some familiar faces further ahead. It was the Swedish family we had met in Mirissa. Despite everything that had happened, a wave of relief washed over me when I saw them, even though they looked as worn and shocked as we felt. The mother, Agneta, had one arm in a cast, wrapped and protected, and the dark circles under her eyes spoke of many sleepless nights. But the most important thing was that they were all alive. We approached them, and after a moment of long, silent embraces and brief, hoarse words of relief, they began to share their story.

Agneta explained that the owners of the bungalows where we had all stayed had also survived, which came as a relief. I felt a bit of the tension in my body release, though the heaviness still lingered. Knowing they had survived felt like a small light in the darkness. She also shared that the French children we used to see running along the beach had survived—but it had been a close call.

"It was the chef, Ravi," she said, her voice filled with gratitude, her eyes welling up with tears as she looked at us. "He took the two little boys by the hand and ran as fast as he could toward the hills. He saved their lives."

Each story felt like a fresh shock, a new reality to absorb. The images of the French boys, laughing and playing on the beach, now contrasted with the thought of them screaming, holding onto the chef's hands as they fled for their lives. My stomach tightened.

Pierre, the father of the French family, had been out surfing when the tsunami hit. Agneta explained how he had miraculously managed to cling to his surfboard and somehow survived the massive waves. It was a story that felt surreal—as if no human could survive such chaos. We stood in silence, trying to comprehend, but some things were beyond our understanding.

Amid these stories of survival, there was also profound tragedy. Agneta shared in a low, trembling voice that the British woman, Margaret, who had been staying in the same bungalows as us, had been found dead in the ruins. And the French mother, Pierre's wife, was still missing. No one had seen her since the waves crashed over the beach, and while the search continued, hope seemed almost entirely lost. We stood there, silently sharing their pain.

"The treehouse that belonged to the surf group... there's nothing left of it," Agneta continued. "They had partied late on Christmas Day, and most likely, everyone was asleep when the waves hit. None of them survived."

Hearing about the young surfers—so alive and free when we last saw them—and now knowing they were gone was overwhelming. I could almost hear their laughter in the back of my mind, hear the music from their party, and I felt the weight of reality sinking deeper into me. This wasn't a nightmare we could wake up from. This was our new reality.

As we stood there, surrounded by survivors at the airport, with people wearing the same empty, exhausted expressions, the magnitude of what we had experienced began to sink in. That we survived was a miracle, but it was also an immense burden. I thought about all the people we had met—the faces now lost forever. The sorrow and relief blended in a way I didn't know how to handle.

We said goodbye to the Swedish family, but as we hugged, we all understood that we were never truly saying farewell. We shared something that no one else could comprehend, a bond forged in one of the most terrifying and tragic experiences of our lives. We knew that none of us would ever forget these days, and we also knew that we would never forget the people we had lost.

We slept on the floor in line, alongside hundreds of other people from different parts of the world. I looked around at the people lying side by side – a strange mix of individuals, all sharing the same goal: to escape the disaster and return to the safety of home. It was a surreal sight: people sleeping on their backpacks, wrapped in clothes they had been wearing for days. No one complained; no one even seemed to notice the discomfort anymore. We had all become accustomed to this new reality.

Several hours later, we were informed that we would be flying to Prague the following day. It would be an evacuation flight for Europeans from various countries. Despite the relief of finally having a way home, there was still a lingering uncertainty in the air. We knew that nothing was certain until we were actually on the plane and in the air.

When we finally boarded the plane and fastened our seatbelts, it felt like we could finally exhale. But it quickly became clear that the journey wouldn't be as straightforward as we had hoped. The plane made a stop in Dubai, but none of us were allowed to disembark. Armed military personnel stood at the doors, watching every movement. It quickly became evident that their job was to ensure no one left the plane – some of us lacked passports and travel documents.

The plane was refueled while we sat there, strapped in and exhausted, as the activity unfolded around us. It was a strange feeling to be so close to another city, another place, yet so far from it. The soldiers stood unwavering at the doors, and it felt as though we were prisoners in our own means of transport, even though we understood that their presence was meant to maintain order.

After what felt like an eternity, we took off again. We knew
we were closer to home, but the sense of surrealism lingered.
It felt as if the world outside had paused while we moved
through it in our armored make-believe bird.

As we finally set course for Prague, the tension that had
gripped us began to ease slightly. The journey home was still
long, but we were one step closer to safety and one step
further from the disaster.

Among the passengers on the plane, there was a silence that
felt almost heavy to bear. A man with a plastered leg sat in
one of the seats ahead of us, with a bandage wrapped around
his head. He groaned softly to himself, as if every movement
caused him pain. Even though we were on our way out of the
disaster zone, it was clear that no one had truly left it behind.
A woman across the aisle sat leaning against the airplane
window, quietly crying. Her shoulders shook slightly as tears
streamed down her face. Everyone onboard bore the scars,
both physical and emotional.

We were all heading toward safety, but none of us could
escape the weight of what we had left behind. The plane
carrying us away was filled with both relief and sorrow, and
though we sat in silence, we were all part of the same tragic
chapter.

TWENTYONE

The next evening, as I put the children to bed, it felt as if the world had come to a halt. I lay in bed between my two little ones, feeling their warm bodies close to mine, their breaths soft and steady. I read from their favorite book, the story they always asked for, even though they already knew it by heart. There was something comforting in the familiar words, something that gently lulled them into a safe, deep sleep.

As I read about the brave little rabbit who faced its fears and embarked on an adventure, I caught a glimpse of my daughter closing her eyes and sleepily smiling. My son, always determined to stay awake until the end, pulled the blanket tighter around himself and rested his head on my arm. I stroked his hair and continued reading in a low, soft voice, almost a whisper.

It suddenly struck me that this was all that truly mattered. The children. Their warmth, their trust. Everything I did, every decision I made, was for them. Their small hands clutching mine filled me with a love so powerful it almost hurt. This moment, this stillness, was what I always wanted to protect.

When the book was finished, I stayed in the darkness for a while, my daughter's head heavy on my shoulder and my son's tiny hand in mine. Their closeness enveloped me with a sense of peace I rarely found elsewhere. They were my everything. And as I sat there, my thoughts began to wander—what kind of life did I want to give them? What did I want them to learn from me? I realized that I no longer wanted them to see me exhausted and trapped in a job that drained me.

In the dim glow of the nightlight, I shifted slightly, kissed them gently on their foreheads, and felt something resolute awaken within me. I would show them what strength looked like—a life where I pursued my dreams and demonstrated what true courage meant.

December 30, 2004
Prag, Tjeckien

When we landed in Prague, the air suddenly felt easier to breathe. For the first time in what felt like forever, we could take a deep breath without the weight of everything we'd been through pressing on us. We were on our way home—home to our safe, calm Sweden. Even though we would need to spend one night in Prague before flying onward, it felt like a mere formality—a final step before we could leave it all behind and return to safety.

But as we stepped out of the arrivals hall, we were met with something entirely unexpected. Cameras clicked incessantly, and microphones were suddenly shoved in our faces. Journalists stood gathered in a pack, shouting questions in Czech, eager to capture a story of survival from the tsunami. Mom, with her exhausted body and heavy heart, resolutely pushed the journalists aside and took Olof and me under each arm. We half-ran out of there, through the bustling airport, desperate for a moment of peace.

Once we finally managed to escape the insistent press, we were approached by another group of people who seemed calmer and friendlier. They handed out leaflets about psychological support, though initially, we couldn't understand the Czech text. When they heard that we weren't locals, they kindly explained in English that psychological help would be available once we got home to process everything we had experienced. It felt like a promise that someone would take care of us, but it was also a reminder that what we had gone through wasn't over just because we were now on solid ground.

When we finally left the airport and arrived at the same worn hotel where we had stayed before heading to Sri Lanka—what felt like an eternity ago—we could finally exhale. It was strange how a place that had once been a mere layover on our way to an adventure now felt like a haven of temporary security.

In the hotel room, I decided to take a shower. As I took off my shirt, Mom gasped. "Oh my gosh, child! What happened to you?" At first, I had no idea what she meant, but then she began to spin me around to inspect my body. I had several large bruises around my arms, ribs, back, and thighs—something I hadn't even noticed until now. "What about the rest of you?" she cried out, checking Dad and Olof as well. It turned out Olof's feet were covered in cuts, and we were all marked with bruises that had gone unnoticed in the chaos. We were in shock at how much our bodies had endured without us realizing it. But despite everything, we were incredibly grateful. We were alive. The worst injuries we had sustained were cuts and bruises—an almost miraculous outcome given everything we had been through.

After my shower, I came out to find Dad watching the TV. The whole family sat silently, glued to the screen. For the first time, we began to grasp the scale of the catastrophe. We had been living in our own bubble of survival, but now we were seeing the hard facts being broadcast to the world: thousands dead, communities destroyed, countless missing, and entire regions obliterated. The numbers scrolled across the screen, with death tolls rising hour by hour.

- **Indonesia**: Near the epicenter, particularly in Aceh. Deaths: Around 170,000 to 220,000.
- **Sri Lanka**: About 1,500 to 1,600 kilometers from the epicenter. Deaths: Around 35,000.
- **India**: About 1,500 to 2,000 kilometers from the epicenter. Deaths: Around 18,000.
- **Thailand**: About 500 to 800 kilometers from the epicenter. Deaths: Around 8,000.
- **Maldives**: About 2,500 kilometers from the epicenter. Deaths: 82.
- **Somalia**: About 4,500 to 5,000 kilometers from the epicenter. Deaths: Around 289.

Seeing these figures was chilling. It was overwhelming to realize how many lives had been lost. We were among the lucky ones. When we landed in Prague and walked through the airport, we had thought the journey home was the final step. But now, sitting there in the hotel, watching the news, we realized that what we had experienced was far larger than we could comprehend.

We stayed glued to the television all evening, switching between BBC and CNN, trying to make sense of what had happened. The news channels repeatedly showed images of the devastation along Asia's shores, but it was an interview with a scientist on CNN that truly helped us begin to understand the tsunami's unimaginable power. The scientist, an older man in a white shirt with deliberate, slow movements, spoke calmly but intensely as he showed images and diagrams to explain what had occurred.

"A tsunami," he explained, pointing to a diagram with red arrows, "is not an ordinary wave driven by the wind. It occurs when massive amounts of water are suddenly displaced, often following an undersea earthquake or volcanic eruption." He paused, and the image showed two large tectonic plates pressing against each other beneath the ocean surface. "When these plates—like in the case of the Indian Ocean earthquake—shift, the water above them moves abruptly and forcefully. In this case, we're talking about billions of tons of seawater displaced upward and outward from the epicenter, primarily in an east-west direction."

"This is one of the most powerful earthquakes ever recorded," the scientist continued. "Its magnitude reached 9.3 on the moment magnitude scale. This earthquake released an incredible amount of energy that spread across the Earth, estimated to be equivalent to 9,560 gigatons of TNT or 550 million Hiroshima bombs. This earthquake has impacted the entire planet," he added.

I couldn't fully grasp what he meant, but I understood it implied an unimaginable force. It felt as though he was describing the end of the world.

The scientist's illustration showed how the massive earthquake had generated waves radiating in all directions. We watched in horror as the graphic depicted the towering waves crashing relentlessly over Indonesia's coastline. The destruction there was absolute—the wave had obliterated nearly everything in its path.

In a voice filled with reverence for the forces of nature, he explained how the waves had traveled across the ocean, carrying the energy released by the earthquake to countries thousands of kilometers away from the epicenter.

"The tremor was felt across almost all of Southeast Asia and triggered smaller earthquakes as far away as Alaska. Some islands off the coast of Sumatra appear to have shifted by up to 20 meters. Even the Earth's rotation and shape are believed to have been slightly affected," the scientist explained.

We sat frozen, watching the dramatic visuals. I found it difficult to fully comprehend the sheer magnitude of the forces that had been unleashed. We had survived. But we were far from alone in our struggle.

We sat there, silent and deeply affected by everything we had just learned. Words failed us.

TWENTYTWO

The next morning, I woke up with a fresh perspective. We had made a decision—a decision to face this together. It felt as though the heavy burden I had been carrying for so long had lifted. Sitting at the kitchen table with a cup of coffee in my hand, I felt new thoughts and possibilities beginning to take shape.

For the first time in a long while, all doors seemed open before me. My thoughts quickly formed into ideas—I could start my own consulting firm. I had the experience, the knowledge, and the drive. I knew I could create something meaningful, something that reflected my own values, where I could contribute without compromising my integrity or anyone else's.

Another thought crept in, something I had dreamed about for years: developing an online store. I could combine it with my consulting business, offering tools and courses, especially for people who wanted to build enterprises that benefited everyone involved. Just the thought of it made my heart beat faster. It was something that had once felt impossible, an idea I had never fully dared to explore.

But now, I was free to try, free to build and run something based on my own values.

Then, as a natural progression, yet another idea emerged: to start coaching people. I wanted to help others at the beginning of their journeys, people with visions but without the right support. Being a mentor and guide felt incredibly meaningful. Helping others grow, supporting them as they developed their ideas—this was something I was passionate about.

But the idea that struck deepest, that went straight to my heart, was the thought of writing down my own story. Everything I had been through, everything I had suppressed, needed to come to light. I thought of my time in Sri Lanka, of the tsunami, and how I had carried those memories as a heavy burden for so many years. Writing wouldn't just be a way to process what I had experienced—it would be my way of understanding and finding healing. I would tell my truth, exactly as I remembered it, and let the words become part of my healing process.

Anticipation bubbled within me. Perhaps I had been living with blinders on, trapped in a world too small for my ideas and ambitions. But now... now anything felt possible.

Yet, one problem remained. Would I have the courage to go back?

December 31, 2004
Landvetter, Sverige

We barely got a wink of sleep that night either. Suddenly, all the bruises I hadn't even noticed before began to ache, and my thoughts spun relentlessly. How could something so horrific happen? I had never been particularly religious, but one thing was clear: if there was a God, he couldn't possibly be kind. The images of twisted faces and broken bodies replayed in my mind over and over, like a bad movie that refused to end. I was torn between relief that we had survived and guilt over the fact that we could just leave it all behind and go home.

Early in the morning of December 31st, we were scheduled to fly home to Sweden, to Landvetter. We boarded a small propeller plane with about twenty other passengers from various parts of the world.

We remained silent throughout the journey, but as we approached Gothenburg and Landvetter, the plane began to sway alarmingly. The pilot announced that the wind had picked up and the landing would be turbulent. And turbulent it was—I'd never been afraid of flying before, but in that moment, fear gripped me. The plane jolted violently, and a meal cart came loose, crashing into the wall. A flight attendant screamed and began crying. It felt like everyone's nerves were on edge. Perhaps she, too, had experienced things in recent days that had shaken her, or perhaps I was interpreting everything as more perilous than it actually was.

When we finally landed, I realized I had been holding my breath the entire time. I exhaled, but the calming sense of safety didn't fully settle in. After we collected our luggage and headed toward the arrivals hall, the tension returned. I started breathing heavily, bracing myself to face journalists and the relentless clicking of cameras. This time, the questions would be in Swedish. Mom took my hand. She was thinking the same thing. We took a deep breath and walked out. I closed my eyes, ready to push through the crowd.

But when I opened my eyes, there were no journalists. No cameras. Instead, there he was—my grandfather, calm as ever. And oh, how glad I was that it was him who had come to pick us up. He said nothing, just hugged us tightly before speaking in his reassuring voice: "Let's go home."

We packed into the car and drove off. We rode in silence until Mom broke it with a worried tone. "We need to take Olof to the health center to have his feet checked. He has cuts, and they could get infected."

When we parked outside the health center, the rest of us waited in the car while Olof got treated. It felt like an eternity before they returned, but eventually, we were back on the road, heading to Grandma's house, where she was waiting with a warm meal. At Grandma and Grandpa's, we finally found the comfort we had been yearning for.

When we got home, the phone rang. It was my best friend. "Oh my God! I heard you got back, something about a wave or whatever. Lucky you weren't in Thailand, it's apparently awful there. I'll pick you up after dinner, and we'll head to the New Year's party!"

A New Year's party? It was New Year's Eve. I hadn't even registered what day it was. I looked at Mom, who nodded at me. "Go out and have some fun, we can talk tomorrow. I'm heading to bed."

I changed and headed out. At my friend's house, the party was in full swing when I arrived. No one dared to ask me outright what had happened, so the conversation remained awkwardly superficial. But after a few beers, one of my schoolmates broke the silence. "So, what happened? Did you see a lot of dead people or something?"

His question was both insensitive and direct, but perhaps it was exactly what was needed to break the awkward tension. Everyone had been avoiding the topic that lingered in the back of their minds. I gave a brief account of what had happened, leaving out much of the detail. I didn't want to relive it all right then and there.

As the clock struck midnight, we went outside to light fireworks. One of the rockets tipped over and hit me square in the stomach. I stumbled backward and fell, but I wasn't hurt. The rocket flew on and exploded beneath a car. Moments later, I was hoisted back to my feet by one of my friends, who exclaimed, "If you survived a tsunami, you're not going to die now!"

I started laughing—a freeing sensation washed over me. "No, I'm invincible," I replied, taking a few deep swigs from a champagne bottle someone handed me. I let myself be swept up in the warm haze of the party, enveloped by the numbing effects of the alcohol.

TWENTYTHREE

I had avoided this moment for twenty years. There had always been too many reasons not to come back, too many obstacles in the way. But now, as I stood at the temple, wrapped in the warm, humid air, nothing could stop me anymore. I had fought to survive, to process, to move on. And now, I was here again.

The temple is just a stone's throw from the bus stop where we stood that day, the day everything changed. Memories flood in—how we were crammed together on the bus, how the panic began to spread like a wave as powerful as the one that would soon hit. It was from this very place that we fought for our lives.

With slow steps, I climb the stairs, one step at a time. My heart pounds, each step heavy with the weight of everything I've carried. The air is thick with incense, and the monks' chants resonate softly, reminding me of something greater than life itself. I pause at the entrance and remove my shoes, an instinctive ritual.

Inside, enveloped by the temple's stillness and scents, I kneel before the altar. My hands tremble as I press them together in silent prayer. What am I praying for, really? Forgiveness? Peace? Or perhaps just a moment of calm after years of emotional storms?

As I sit there, something soft, almost warm, begins to spread through my body. I survived. I made it back here, and now—stronger than ever. Slowly, I rise and wipe away a solitary tear. So many tears I've shed for this place over the years. What's one more? I gaze out over the temple grounds. The sun shines high in the sky, casting a golden light over the garden, and the area is surrounded by a serene stillness.

But the journey isn't over. I have one final task, one last meeting. With a deep breath and a lighter heart, I turn and descend the temple's stairs. The path to Sumudu and her daughters feels like the natural continuation of this journey. It's time to see them again, to thank them, and to create new memories—not to replace the old ones, but to honor them.

EPILOGUE

The tsunami of December 26, 2004, struck Matara on Sri Lanka's southern coast around 9:10 in the morning. First came a wave surging along the coastline, but just ten minutes later, a second, significantly larger wave struck. It hit the city mercilessly, leaving total devastation in its wake. I remember the ground shaking, and it felt as if the entire world was falling apart, but it wasn't until later that we understood the scale of the force that had struck us.

The worst-hit areas were the southern and eastern coasts of the island. Waves as high as 12 meters destroyed everything in their path, surging up to 2 kilometers inland. The official death toll today stands at approximately 35,000. Some estimates place the total number of deaths (confirmed dead and missing) at nearly 39,000. Among the victims were 1,700 passengers who perished when a train on a bridge or embankment was swept away, marking the worst train disaster in history.

Sri Lanka's government deployed 20,000 soldiers for rescue efforts and to prevent looting. The material damage was immense, and it was estimated that around 1 million people were left homeless.

Beyond the immediate destruction, the tsunami brought with it tons of sand and silt that covered the ground, destroyed crops, and blanketed roads and houses. Saltwater seeped deep into wells and irrigation systems, causing a rapid shortage of freshwater. Many coastal communities still face significant challenges in restoring their agricultural land, where salt deposits continue to hinder cultivation.

The country, which had already been grappling with a prolonged civil war between the Sinhalese majority and the Tamil minority, found itself in a new, shared crisis. The disaster temporarily united different communities, but it also led to new conflicts over where aid should be directed and how it should be distributed. In areas controlled by the LTTE – the Tamil Tigers – tensions arose as aid organizations attempted to reach the affected, and the LTTE sought to control incoming relief.

Meanwhile, rescue efforts continued, both by the Sri Lankan government and the international community. Indian military helicopters transported the injured to naval ships stationed along the coast. International aid filled the ports with ships loaded with supplies and medicine. The first days were marked by chaos and desperation, but a slow recovery began to take shape, though it could never replace the lives that were lost.

Sri Lanka was hit hard, but so were other countries around the Indian Ocean. Indonesia, located directly next to the epicenter, suffered the greatest losses, both from the tsunami waves and the earthquake itself. It is estimated that approximately 230,000 people died or went missing there, with vast material destruction.

I have often reflected on how unfair it feels to have experienced something so devastating and then be able to leave it behind. While we were fortunate enough to return to the safety of Sweden, so many others were left to face a shattered reality. I feel a deep sense of guilt toward those who stayed behind and toward the families who lost their loved ones.

But perhaps that guilt is best carried with the understanding that stories like these must be shared, to remember the lives that were lost and to highlight the courage and humanity that arose in the shadow of catastrophe.

I will always carry a part of Sri Lanka with me, a part that is both light and dark. It serves as a reminder of nature's power, of what truly matters, and of life's fragility.

Thank you!

Writing this book has been a journey in itself, and I could not have done it without the support of the wonderful people around me.

A heartfelt thank you to Åsa and Helena, who, with their meticulous eyes and wisdom, proofread and helped bring this text to life.

Thank you to my parents, who, with their invaluable contributions and memories, added details that made the story even richer and more vivid. And to my brother – thank you for always being there; your presence and support mean everything.

A special thank you to my husband, who tirelessly supports all my projects and ideas. You are my rock in everything I do. And to my wonderful children – you give me the strength to dare, to believe in myself, and to never give up.

This book would not have been possible without you. Thank you from the bottom of my heart.